THE FAIRY QUEEN

THE OBSIDIAN SPINDLE SAGA

BOOK THREE

RUSSELL NOHELTY

SPECIAL THANKS

Adriane Ruzak, Amanda Jackson, Angela, Anthony Bachman, Caledonia, Caspar Williams, Celeste and Bryan Cornish, Chad Bowden, Chris Call, Chris Meeson, Christopher C Epping, Christopher Prew, CJ Ives Lopez, Daniel Biittner, Daniel Groves, Dave Baxter, Dave Goldberg, David Chamberlain, David Drummond, David Straube, Desiree Duffy, DJ Inzeo, Ed S, Edward Nycz Jr., Emerson Kasak, Erin Congdon, Gabriella Farmer, Gary Phillips, Hannah Long, Hollie Buchanan II, Jeff Lewis, Jennifer & Charlie Geer, John C. Heller, Johnny Britt, Jon Tugan, Joshua Bowers, Joshua Pantalleresco, Juli, Kimberly Herout, Larry Gilman, Lincoln City Archery, Lisa Homolka, Lisa Lyons, Matthew Johnson, Maxi Organ, Melissa Showers, Michael Kingston, Michael Perler, Mike Jones, Monkey King Comics, Nic Nelson, Nick Smith, Paul Rose Jr., Per Stalby, Rachel Adams, Rhel ná DecVandé, Richard A Williams, Rob MacAndrew, Rowan, S.A. McClure, Salvatore Puma, Scott Kilburn, Stephen Ballentine, Steven "Waffles" Lane, Taiga Char, Talinda Willard (everfai), Victoria Nohelty, and Walter Weiss

The Fairy Queen
Book 3 of the Obsidian Spindle Saga

By:
Russell Nohelty

Edited by:
Leah Lederman

Proofread by:
Katrina Roets

Cover by:
JV Arts

Formatting by:
Turbo Kitten Industries

CHAPTER 1
AINE

Everyone of royal blood needed to die before my reign as queen over the Land of Oz could truly begin. Every single one of Nimue's sycophants would have to be disposed of so we didn't have a repeat of what happened to Rose, the last queen. I would not be assassinated. I'd lived too long and seen too much to get taken down like that.

"You can't do this!" Cyrano said, tears falling down his long, ugly nose. His piteous, bloodshot eyes stared at me with a combination of contempt and nervousness.

"I can do whatever I want," I snarled. "I am the queen. Or have you forgotten that already?"

Cyrano and his accomplices were responsible for Rose's death. She'd only been queen for about eleven seconds before they killed her, and I wouldn't let them get away with it. She was my friend. The ancillary benefit was that their deaths led me directly to the most powerful throne in Urgu, but that was just a fortuitous coincidence.

"Please," Odysseus sobbed. He was the tall and strapping master of war, crying like a child. Even hundreds of years of life didn't prepare him for his own death. "Have some heart."

I nearly laughed. "Did you have heart when you plotted to kill the rightful queen of Oz?"

I had already sent the council of bishops from the Church of the Six to their deaths over the edge of the royal balcony. Ozma, a previous queen, used to address her adoring subjects there. That was before she was usurped and then eventually thrown from the same balcony by the one who had deposed her, the wicked witch. Nimue.

The council, along with the Church's leader, had led the charge to kill Rose. Grand Pious Edwina plunged the dagger into the poor girl's back herself, and then had the audacity to smile afterward. They had to die first, to send a message. Nobody dared kill the clergy. After all, the Church of the Six served all Urgu, not just the Land of Oz, and I had wiped them off the face of the continent with nary a second thought.

Once the bishops were gone, I had dusted the entirety of the royal court for all the Emerald City to witness. They cheered for it. The Church of the Six was an antiquated institution and the nobles had held down the masses for too long. Now, all that was left for me to do was to finish the small council and then I could start rebuilding the Land of Oz.

"We didn't mean to do it." Antonio, master of coin, sniffled as he looked at the crowd of Ozians screaming for his head. "We were doing what was best for Oz!"

"Don't insult my intelligence," I spat back at him. "I was a queen since before I came to this place and have ruled the Enchanted Woods for centuries. Do you really think I know not how to take care of conspirators?" I knew the people demanded blood. They craved it. Nimue knew that, and I had tried to impart that advice to Rose, but the girl didn't believe me, and it led to her death. She was too kind-hearted to rule.

"We didn't—" Cyrano almost lost his footing from atop the railing where he stood precariously. "We weren't..."

"What?" I asked. Rose was my only friend, the only person who had treated me kindly in decades, and I would have my revenge for her. I would solidify my rule. "Expect to be caught?"

"We were just doing what was best for Oz," Odysseus pleaded, snot bubbling in his nose. "Can't you see that?"

"Yes, I can see that you truly believe the lie," I said, floating above them. My small size would have been comical compared to their stature if I didn't ooze power from every pore. I knew how to command a room. We fae had to learn quickly about the true dastardly nature of humans passed down from generation to generation. If we didn't, we would be subject to witness it firsthand. "The worst part is that you won't admit your treachery and die with dignity."

I looked each counselor in the eye, the purple of my robes reflected in each conspirator's face. My mother thought that my choice of purple would make me look soft, but I knew it projected royalty. "And wasn't it convenient that what was best for Oz happened to be the best for your coffers?"

"That was a coincidence!" Antonio shouted. "The girl could not rule. You saw it. She was a child, and an outsider. She had no knack for—"

"We were all outsiders once!" I bellowed. "She was chosen by Hypnos himself, and decreed to rule by divine right until..." The thought of Rose's body deteriorating into ash stopped me, momentarily. I lifted my chin, maintaining my air of invincibility. I could not choke up, not now. And there was nothing more to say. I gave a nod to the Mountain People who held sharp lances to the backs of the former small council. "Drop them."

The Mountain People that Red and Chelle rescued from the Gates of Droangor proved to be most loyal after Rose's assassination. They were instrumental in rounding up the nobles who begged sanctuary from the Queen's Guard and provided insulation from the Queen's guard that was still inexplicably loyal to Nimue. Plus, their monstrous appearance made even the most battle-hardened soldier quiver. Those that plotted murder thought twice before crossing me, as I had my own army of elite soldiers protecting me.

My Mountain soldiers turned their glowing eyes to me and nodded back. They pushed their lances into the backs of the sniveling conspirators, who fell off the balcony with a collective scream. They tumbled through the air and smashed against the ground, breaking into a million pieces of ash on the cobblestone courtyard.

I watched the citizens of the Emerald City cheering as the men's ashes floated into the air. "Justice for your queen!" I shouted, and again the crowd erupted with cheers. They chanted my name, over and over again. The rapturous joy on their faces proved their loyalty to me. I rode into their hearts on the strings of Rose's kind soul. The common people loved Rose for toppling the Wicked Witch and were heartbroken when she was murdered.

In their grief, I brought stability. I had mentored Rose and trained her to become a queen during her short days on the throne. They knew me as a fair, if not feared ruler, and I swore to bring justice to their beloved queen. Yes, I took the throne when Rose died, but the people of Oz let me keep it. I was their queen. There was no one besides me who had a claim to it, since I'd killed all of them. Until Hypnos appointed a new ruler—which had taken over a hundred years the last time around—I would rule the land.

"A new era of wonder has begun!" I shouted to the crowd. "Long live the Emerald City!"

The throne of Oz had never been my birthright, but its power was something I coveted in my youth. The Enchanted Woods had its charm, but Oz was the most powerful province in Urgu, and in lieu of escaping the Dream Realm outright, it was a fine prize. Where Rose, the Dreamer, had failed to control the nobles, and the Wicked Witch had failed to open the Obsidian Spindle, I would be successful. I had secured justice for Rose, my friend, and now I would journey through the Obsidian Spindle to my destiny, my return to Earth.

I had seen the door open once, only once, for a single shining moment when the Gorgon, Chelle, walked inside it with her beloved Rose's ashes. The door shut behind her. Now I knew it could be opened with the right spell, and Nimue knew the spell. I would find her, even if it took a century, and make my way back to Earth, and away from Urgu forever.

"*FAIRY!*" a voice boomed. "*Meet your end.*"

Black ooze inked through the sky like oil creeping across water, until the sky was sackcloth black and the wind began to howl. Below, the citizens of Oz screamed and fled in all directions. We had all heard the voice before.

Hera.

She was on her way to destroy the land of Oz and take the Obsidian Spindle by force. An onyx mist rose into the air and crashed through the street like a tidal wave, sweeping up my subjects in its wake.

Shadow Demons. Hera controlled them. They would

destroy everything. I would be nothing but a queen of ashes.

Before Rose died, she had raised the defenses on the castle. No magical being that meant to do me harm could enter the castle without my permission.

I just had to hope it was powerful enough to keep out a god.

CHAPTER 2
CHELLE

Bang!

Bang!

Bang!

My fists had been scraped raw from slamming them against the door to the Obsidian Spindle for hours, but the door wouldn't budge, even an inch. My blood smeared across the oaken door as I slammed against it. "Let me out!

"*Magna augue!*" I shouted. A fireball swelled between my hands. It grew to the size of a basketball before I pushed it out toward the door, where it exploded without leaving so much as a scratch. I smelled my burning blood as it dissipated, mixed with the sweet smell of smoke as the remnants of the extinguished flame floated into the darkness of the Spindle that was my prison.

"*Fulgur inspiratione!*" A blue shock of lightning grew from my fingertips, and I flung it at the door like I was Emperor Palpatine. The lightning shook my hands, but I didn't let up for a full minute, and when I was done, the only thing left to show my effort was a black stain of electricity on the door.

There was no way to open the door back to Urgu. Between my endless sessions sewing the Quilt of Life together with the other fates, Clotho and Lachesis, I would come to the door and try to open it, desperate to end my obligation to the Gorgon women who held me in the Obsidian Spindle.

"I am a hostage," I muttered.

"You aren't a hostage," I heard from behind me. I turned to see Clotho standing on the black stairs, her ancient snakes coiled silently around her head. She smiled at me. "If you were a hostage, then we would send for ransom from somebody who cares about you. The only two who care about you here are my sister and me. And you are not a prisoner either, since you chose to remain here with us."

"Semantics." It was true, though: I had entered a contract with them and become a fate after their sister Atropos was murdered by Nimue. That crazy witch opened the Obsidian Spindle for the first time in a century, and what did she do but kill one of the fates?

"We are also stuck here, and that is an appropriate term. The three of us, stuck together, after having made a choice."

Only a Gorgon could become a fate, and I just happened to be Gorgon enough to fit the bill after the death of their sister, Atropos. Wrong place at the wrong time, or right place at the right time, depending on how you looked at it, and who was doing the looking.

"I just want to go home."

"You are home," Clotho said, sweetly. I liked her more than her ornery sister, but I saw myself in Lachesis. I think she saw herself in me, too, which was why she was so hard on me. Clotho was kind.

It was an easy choice, to become a fate, because it saved Rose, the woman I loved more than life itself, and sent her back to Earth. If I hadn't made that choice, the door back to Earth couldn't be opened, and Rose would be damned to ashes for eternity.

Now, at least she was back on Earth where she was safe and could live a real life. I would die for that girl, so the least I could do was suffer through the mindless tedium of sewing the Quilt of Life for an epoch or two.

"I hate it here."

"That's how it felt for us, too," Clotho said. "But in time, you grow to love the isolation, and the quiet." Clotho held her hand out. "Come, we have a surprise for you."

"I've seen your surprises," I replied. "I haven't liked one yet."

I looked down at my fingers, bloody and raw from a combination of banging on the door to the Spindle and working the needle and thimble for days on end. Gingerly, I placed my hand in hers.

"You will like this one, I believe," Clotho said. She led me up the stairs.

That was how it had been since I came to them. They asked questions as statements and expected me to follow them blindly. I had never followed anything blindly in my entire life. I never believed in the will of gods, or the fickle finger of fate, even though I was now one of them.

I was no willing subject. I meant what I said. The fact that I couldn't leave meant I was a prisoner. Even though I had made this choice, I regretted it. Only thoughts of Rose made it worthwhile, and the belief that she was safe. I held onto those thoughts and that belief every time the regret overwhelmed me.

"None have ever taken the mantle of fate willingly," Clotho said, walking up the dark stairwell that led to the Spindle's only room at the top. That was where Clotho spun the thread of another lonely soul bound for the afterlife, and Lachesis knit it into a patch. It was my job to take the patch and sew it into the Quilt of Life.

"Why did you choose to stay?" I asked Clotho.

"Similar to you, actually," she replied. "Though it was a boy. He was very sick, and my sacrifice kept him alive, for a time. They all die, eventually. I remember the day Lachesis weaved his patch, just like she weaved those of the ones she had loved and hoped to save. It was the last time I shed a tear until the death of my sister."

"That's sad," I replied.

"Quite," Clotho nodded. "But in time, I grew to love the work. It is important, and there are so few truly important jobs. I take satisfaction in that, and in the simple act of remembering the dead, and my part in all of it."

"That doesn't sound like much," I said.

"It's not much, but it is all we have." Clotho walked into the room. When I followed, she sat to the left of her sister, Lachesis, who was silently putting another patch together. Next to her was a stack of patches, waiting for me. I looked down at them. Maybe she was right. Maybe there was joy in it, at least in the duty of it. Each of those pieces represented a life, and their memory would always live on in the Quilt of Life.

"Sit," Clotho said with a smile.

I shook my head. "I don't know if I can sew any more today."

"That is not your choice," Lachesis said. Her voice was hoarse. "Sit. Down."

She treated me like a mule to break, and it often took all of my willpower not to burn her to ash like Nimue had done to her sister. "You talk a big game for an old woman. Remember, I have a body, which makes me the most powerful thing in this room. I could take you both."

I was the only being in all Urgu with a body. Everyone else came through in their dreams, as a soul, or as the result of an overactive imagination, but I came through a door guarded by Mydnyte, a servant of Nox, the goddess of darkness.

Clotho chuckled. "You should not underestimate us, but we will not force you. Nothing will force you, but a feeling, deep in your soul, will compel you to finish the job we started, eventually."

"You mock everything we stand for," Lachesis added. "Atropos—"

"Died," I said. "She died to make room for me. I know. And you hate it. I know that. I still don't understand why, though."

Clotho smiled. "We will tell you. But first, we have a gift for you."

I eyed her suspiciously. "I don't know what you could give me that I want."

"We have many powers you have not seen," Lachesis said.

"And we will teach you one," Clotho said. "We will teach you how to reach out and see your beloved."

"Rose?" An excited shudder rolled through me.

"Yes," Lachesis said. "But be warned. Do not dwell in the land of the living, or you will be lost, and see things that you do not wish to see. The memories will wash over you, and you will be overwhelmed by what you will witness."

"I can handle it," I said. "I've seen—"

"You've seen nothing," Lachesis snapped. "Atropos was wrong to give up her life for you, and Clotho is wrong to keep you close. You are far too hot-headed for the work we require."

"But she is perfect for what will come next," Clotho said. "It has been foreseen."

"What is next?" I asked, throwing my hands in the air. I had pieced together enough to know that something big was coming, and I had a part in it. "Will you please just tell me instead of talking in riddles?"

"Soon," Clotho replied. "But first, we will show you that which you seek above all else."

I sat down on the mat next to Lachesis. What I wanted more than anything was to see Rose, and if this was a chance, I would listen.

"Close your eyes," Lachesis said. I did.

"Reach out with your feelings and think of Rose. Think of her and let your feelings for her wash over you. Let the most powerful memory of your time together drown you in its happiness."

I thought back to the first time Rose ever saw the snakes that hissed above my head. I was as frightened as I had ever been. Fighting legions of monster hunters didn't make me a fraction as nervous as I was when I came out to her as a monster. No mortal human had ever seen my greatest shame—my truest self. What if she recoiled in horror? I would be forced to start a new life.

But she didn't scream or run away. She simply smiled, and touched them each in turn, sweetly, before turning to me. "They're beautiful," she said. "And so are you."

Tears flowed down my face, and suddenly the dark behind my eyes washed away, and Rose's face stared back at me. Not the memory of Rose, but her actual face. I don't know how I could tell that it wasn't a memory, or a hallucination, but I knew it was real. She was alive, and she was okay.

For the first time in days, I smiled.

CHAPTER 3
ROSE

I wanted to hate myself, my life. I wanted to hate Chelle. I wanted to hate something; anything. Even the littlest thing in the whole world.

But I didn't. I couldn't.

I didn't hate anything. I didn't love anything, either. I didn't feel...anything. Ever since returning from the Dream Realm, I hadn't felt one iota of pain or joy. I had no feelings about moving back in with my parents, or having to commute to school, or selling the van that Chelle and I lived in for almost a year. It still smelled like her when I dropped it off.

I almost thought I could feel something then for a fleeting moment, but as quickly as the feeling came upon me, it drifted away. Even that feeling, strong as it should have come to wreck me, never came too close to the surface. It was like a distant acquaintance on a faraway beach, waving to you from the horizon. You could place a hint of recognition on their face, but you had no real memory of them. That was how the most intense feeling came upon me now.

All I could do was look upon my life with dispassionate inhumanity, as if I wasn't the one living my life, but a bystander watching a boring movie, hoping for it to be over soon. I barely recognized myself in the mirror. My eyes were dull and colorless, except for the blood red veins that splintered from my irises. My dark blonde hair fell onto my face like an ugly mat, and I barely had the energy to brush it away before turning from the mirror and putting on a pair of dirty blue jeans to compliment my stained t-shirt.

I had to take on summer school so that I didn't fall behind on my class load. The world had moved on, even if mine came to a dead stop when I fell into that diabetic coma. It seemed like a lifetime ago I'd been in Urgu.

All in all, I had been in the Dream Realm for less than a month. Upon my return, it took the rest of the semester before I felt well enough to venture outside the house, and by then I had registered an incomplete in all my classes.

At least going to school got me out of the house.

I stepped out of the double wide trailer I shared with my parents and out into the yard, if you could call it that. It was mostly a dirt patch with two fold-out chairs and a small grill we sometimes used to cook hot dogs.

"Off so soon?" my mother said, coming around the side of the trailer where she was hanging clothes on the line. I didn't need to be able to feel, to remember that I hated her. The memories were strong with the misery she put me through. Still, it was only the memory of a feeling, and not the feeling itself.

"Yeah," I said. "Got class."

My parents agreed to add me back to their insurance when I told them that Chelle was gone. Luckily, too, otherwise I would have to pay tens of thousands of dollars in medical bills for my stay in the hospital. They never let me forget it. Every time I tried to avoid them, they made sure I knew that the only reason I wasn't drowning in debt was because of them.

"Don't be too late," Mom said. "I worry. You know, after what we went through this year."

As if them kicking me out of their house was my fault. It wasn't my fault I was gay. It was their fault they disowned me because of it, and now they thought that because Chelle is stuck in the Dream Realm it meant I wasn't gay anymore, like they can just sweep it all under the rug.

Out of sight, out of mind I guess, and I would never tell them differently. I would never tell them anything ever again. I needed a place to stay for now, but once I could pull my life together, I was gone, forever.

"I won't," I lied. I had no idea when I would be home. Hopefully, I would never come home again.

Mom's eyes narrowed. "I got next month's insulin for you when you get back."

Insulin. I needed it, and it cost hundreds of dollars a month without their insurance. I tried to live without it once...and I ended up in a diabetic coma, clinging to life, while my soul was stuck in the Dream Realm.

"K," I said with all the passion I could muster, which was basically none. The implication was clear: If I didn't come home early, I wouldn't get my medicine. If I didn't get my medicine, I would die. Great mom. Little did she know I had a stash that I kept at school in case I decided to run away and never come back. I used the cash from selling the van to make sure I had an escape plan.

I wished that I could fry her with a bolt of lightning, or a fireball, or manipulate her mind, but I no longer had powers. Chelle saw to that when she sent me back to Earth. I was back to being a nothing burger from nowhereville, instead of a Queen with magic bestowed by the gods...and the worst part of it all was that I didn't even have Chelle. She left me alone, in worse shape than when I left.

A twinge of hatred washed over me, then blew away as fast as it came. I was left alone with my nothingness, staring at my mother. I jumped into the beat-up Civic hatchback I'd bought with the money from the van—what was left after buying an emergency stash of insulin—and lumbered off down the dirt road.

CHAPTER 4

RED

I couldn't stay in the castle, or the Land of Oz, once Aine took over. I had been wholly committed to the royal line of Oz for over two hundred years, but I just couldn't stomach it anymore, not with all the political intrigue Aine would surely bring. After the church's betrayal of Rose, I ended my commitment to the royal line and set out for the only being that could bring balance to Urgu: Hypnos.

He still existed somewhere in The Dream Realm. He had to. He had granted his power to Rose once, which meant he still had some connection to the Dream Realm, and he was trapped somewhere he could not escape. No matter how long I had to wander, I would find him and force him to take his place ruling Oz, with a true queen under him to carry out his dictums.

Aine was not the rightful queen, but she was not a usurper, either. Not in the technical sense, at least. Until Hypnos returned to bless another with his throne, there would be no true ruler, and I didn't have the energy to fight for another queen.

"The boat will come for us soon," Boudica said next to me.

Boudica was the queen of the Mountain people, even though the Celtic goddess Agrona technically had never bestowed a blessing on anyone. Boudica earned her way to her crown through defense of her land and service to her people; she kept it by being doggedly loyal to them.

She was one of only two people left in Urgu I trusted, and I had convinced her to join me. The other person I trusted was Balor, but he chose to stay in the Emerald City, defend its people and its queen, and eke out a better life a little at a time. Even though Aine was not the rightful ruler of Oz, Balor thought her a far cry better than any of the other nobles, and trusted her to rule fairly, or at least more fairly than the other choices.

He had seen her with Rose and believed her heart to be true. She was one of only two in the whole coronation who were not found to be conspiring against her. That wasn't much of an endorsement, since the only other who was not conspiring was Nimue, the Wicked Witch, and she had sent all of Oz into darkness for a century.

Boudica saw the value in my quest, and for the good of all Urgu chose to accompany me past the Wall of Itherium. She knew more theories about where Hypnos might be hidden than anyone. The Mountain People were travelers and storytellers. They were large and menacing, the perfect mercenaries, and they returned to the Mountains with tales from all corners of Urgu. Boudica made sure she heard all of those stories.

"I hate the Sandlands," I said.

I knew, though, that of all the places in Urgu, most stories of Hypnos's disappearance came from the Sandlands. I had traveled there before searching for the Cave of

Wonder, Hypnos's supposed resting place, but always came up empty.

Legend had it that Hypnos was contained in a small lamp that prevented him from escaping unless it were rubbed by a human. The only people with memory of the cave were Sekhmet's people of the Sands, who moved across the Earth like the wind, never bound to one place, ever shifting in the desert breeze.

"I have been to the Sandlands before, Boudica, and only left with sand in every crevice. How certain are you of this information?"

"Hrm," Boudica grumbled. "Even information from the most trustworthy source may not be accurate, as is the way of these things."

"My last time in the Sandlands, Shaina and I barely left with our lives."

Shaina was one of the fiercest warriors in all the Sandlands, or she was until she was dusted. She ended up at the right hand of the Soothsayer, the most powerful sorcerer of the Mountain People. We'd tried desperately to find the cave, but came up empty even after a year of searching, and I turned my attention to the Bogs, and the Dark Domain, before returning to Ozma's service in the Land of Oz.

"You are a noble warrior," Boudica said. "But you are not a natural tracker."

I scoffed. "I am an excellent tracker."

"Perhaps in Oz, but to me you are barely competent. The sands move like an organism. They do not stay still for anyone, and only a master tracker can find their way to their destination."

"I had Shaina."

Boudica laughed. "She was young and impetuous. You can tell because she was dusted. I am as old as the mountains, and I have been tracking since I was young here. Trust me, I will bring us to the Cave of Wonder."

"If it exists. I have very little faith we will find anything."

"Everything is faith, Belle. Everything."

I smiled. I liked when she said my name. So few did. So few knew it, even if most knew my story, or some distortion of it told throughout the years. Those who knew I was the same Belle of legend had a habit of dying. All except for Balor.

Still, Balor chose his side, as did the Mountain People. They had been saved by Aine and given clemency by Rose, so they had a great and powerful reason to stay loyal to the queen, whoever she was, and however ill gotten her gains. Even Boudica could not convince them to leave the Emerald City to join us, especially when she told them her next journey would lead them past the Wall of Itherium. They had just escaped the Sandlands and the horrors of the Mountains and had no desire to return.

That left me with Boudica, who believed that Hypnos would bring order back to Urgu, and end the horrors of the Mountains, so she and her people could return home to their beloved realm.

"Come," Boudica said. "The boat comes into port, and we must be on it or risk a week waiting for the next one."

In the distance, a ship rose and crashed down over the waves of the dunes. It was a large wooden vessel, built to navigate the quicksand that separated the Sandlands from Oz. Boudica led us down the hill toward the dock. A skinny man with a long beard and cane held up his arms as we walked closer, signaling for us to stop. He had horns like a ram, a short beard braided down his chin, and eyes like a snake.

"Halt!" the man said. "What business do you have in the Sandlands?"

"Our business is our own," Boudica replied.

"I'm afraid that is not good enough. Enemies of Sekhmet come from the north, and we must protect our borders."

"Enemies? From the Mountains?"

"Yes," the man said, pointing to Boudica's red eyes and the purple neon strands that festooned her hair. "And you are clearly from there."

Only the Mountain people had neon in their hair and glowing eyes. Only they wore all black leather from their shoulders to their feet, with wide armor to make them seem broader and more intimidating than they were in reality; it was a cunning illusion that brought fear to enemies and allies alike.

"We wish no quarrel with the Sandlands," I replied. "We are on a quest."

"A quest?" the man said. "And what be this quest?"

Boudica shook her head for me to stop, but I continued. "We seek the Cave of Wonder."

"The Cave of Wonder?" the man scoffed. "Then you search for lies. You would do well to turn back now."

"You've heard of it?" I asked.

"Nothing but ghost stories. Tales of treasure and magic throughout, and hogwash."

"Be that as it may," Boudica said, "we wish to enter the Sandlands and search for ourselves. We are not enemies of your people."

I pulled a bag of dreams from my pocket, the currency of Urgu. I picked the shiniest pink ball and held it up to him. Inside the ball spun an image of a little girl playing in snow. A common dream, at a time when finding dreams was uncommon. "We offer a dozen dreams like this one for passage across the Quick Sea."

The man bent to inspect the ball. "That is a high price. Ten times more than the cost."

I nodded. "I ask that you bring us over by ourselves, and you speak of this to nobody, not even your closest confidant. This price buys your silence."

"And no questions," Boudica added. "All we want to hear is a 'yes' coming from your mouth. For every other word, we will reduce our price. Understood?"

The man nodded. "Yes."

"Good," Boudica replied as the boat glided into port. "Then lead the way."

CHAPTER 5
NIMUE

At first, I struggled against the darkness of the Nightmare Realm seeping into every part of my vision, but eventually, I succumbed to it. When I let it fill my sight, my eyes focused, and small dots of neon made faint constellations in the sky. The same neon graced some of the bushes speckling the ground. A purple squirrel with swirling eyes skittered across the tree line, and in the distance a hawk shrieked.

Even with shreds of light, the darkness was stifling. Each step weighed heavier on me, dragging me closer to the ground, and leaving me with little will to carry on, and less air to breathe, as if a great boot pressed on my chest.

"*Lux!*" I shouted, and my hand lit, but even with the light from my hand, I could barely see a foot in front of me. The light worked more toward a beacon to find me than protection from the things that went bump in the night. I felt them skittering past, their hot breath on my neck. Something hunted me but I could not make it out, and the thought of it drove every hair on my body to stand on end.

I hid the fear bubbling up from the recesses of my soul. I could not show that I was inches from going mad, or I would surely be seen as prey. Predators hunted the weak, and were I to admit weakness, then I would surely be gobbled up. The only thing that kept me alive was the novelty of my entrance into the Nightmare Realm.

None had ever stepped foot from the Dream Realm to the Nightmare Realm like I had. None would dare even try, unless they were a special brand of crazy, or they had exceptional raw power.

I checked both criteria.

The Fates gave me the power of a god, but since I was not blessed by one, I had a short time to use it before that power ripped my body apart. I had to use my powers and have them rip my body apart, or turn to a new god for a blessing. I refused to ever be powerless again.

"*Lux!*" I shouted, the fire flickering brighter in my hand. My hand stung in pain every time I used magic.

The fates didn't tell me that the more I used my power, the quicker my body burned through it. Every spell I cast drained my life force away. I begged Agrona to give me her blessing, but instead she only allowed me to use her portal to the Nightmare Realm. If I could free her love, Epiales, the god of Nightmares, from whatever spell bound him to the Nightmare Realm, he would grant me a wish.

It was my only chance, so I took it.

Though she didn't say it outright, it was clear that Epiales and Agrona were taking the disappearance of Hypnos as an excuse to conquer the Dream Realm, and I couldn't care less. Let the Dream Realm burn for all I cared, as long as I found a way to protect my power and make it back to Earth, the dream that had consumed me for an eon.

"My, my, my," a deep voice growled in the darkness. "Aren't you a Firestarter? Quite literally, too."

"Funny," I said. A chill ran down my spine, but I refused to give an inch to the voice in the darkness.

"You know…" it took a long pause. "Because of the fire in your hand."

"Yes, I am aware of the fire in my hand."

"You are powerful," the voice said. "I have followed you for a long time. Most would be mad by now."

"I am furious," I replied. "That is the fire that fuels me."

"That's not the mad I meant," the voice said with a giggle. In the darkness, a set of white teeth smiled, then a pair of yellow eyes popped open above them. The sight might have frightened others, but I had been in the service of Hera for generations. She loved to use the darkness as her shroud. "But you knew that already."

"I did," I said.

"We are all mad here," the mouth said with a whimsical melody. "You should join us."

"Have you seen Epiales?" I asked, already tired of the game.

The eyes narrowed. "He is a dear friend of mine. I had tea with him just last week. I would be happy to guide you to him, if you can find it in your heart to trust me."

"Trust you? In this place? You really must be mad."

"I am," the mouth said. "But so are you, after all. Otherwise, you would have never come here without a plan, or a map."

"I have a plan," I replied.

"Sure," the voice said. "To wander aimlessly in the darkness, hoping not to be eaten. Hoping your pitiful power will protect you even as they grow weaker with each passing step?"

"My power is not pitiful!" I screamed. "LIGHTNING!"

Lightning crackled in my fingers, and I let a bolt of it fly toward the mouth, which disappeared, untouched. I saw the heaving chests of a hundred demons reflected in the brief light, and my knees clattered together despite my air of invincibility.

"Tsk, tsk, tsk," the mouth said. "That kind of thing might be impressive where you come from, but here..." the mouth flickered out and reappeared moments later in front of my face. "It is nothing. We eat magic like yours for breakfast."

"Very well," I gulped. "I have rethought your offer, and I accept."

"Wonderful," the mouth replied. "While you are with me, none will dare bother you."

"Why?" I asked, following the mouth through the darkness.

"They will assume you are my pet, and none would dare cross me, as I love my pets more than anything in the universe."

CHAPTER 6
CHELLE

I smiled, watching Rose go about her day in the vision Clotho and Lachesis gave to me. It truly was a gift to see her again, and with it, even my imprisonment did not feel so bad.

I hadn't smiled since I put Rose's ashes inside the golden door and sent her back to Earth, hoping she would be all right. The truth was, I had no idea what would happen. Seeing her alive was everything. No, her life wasn't perfect, but she had one, and that was because of me. I sent her back to Earth. I had given her a second chance, and now she had her whole life to live.

"It is time to go," Lachesis whispered in my ear.

"No," I said, watching Rose drive her new car down the street back to school. "Just another minute. Please."

Clotho whispered into my other ear. "If you stay too long, you will be lost forever."

And then, as if a prophesy, Rose's face melted into a crying heap. She stopped the car on the side of the road and fell onto her dashboard.

"What's happening?" I asked, but there was no answer.

Rose's face dissolved into that of my mother, shrouded in the black of the Nightmare Realm. A loud crack pierced the air and her face contorted into a pained expression. Then she vanished. Darkness flowed over the Dream Realm, and a thousand dead-eyed monsters charged through the streets of the Emerald City.

"The future comes upon us like a wave," Clotho whispered in my ear. "You will drown in it, if you do not leave now."

There was another loud crash, but this time it did not come from my vision. I opened my eyes and was back in the Spindle. The entirety of the Spindle shook and crashed, and then again, the quakes grew faster and more intense.

"What is happening?" I shouted.

"An attack," Clotho said, without a hint of fear.

"Attack!" I pushed myself up from the ground. "Who's attacking us?"

"It was bound to happen." Lachesis shrugged. "Hera is on the rampage."

"Hera!" I said, looking around wildly. "What do we do?"

"There is nothing to do," Clotho said. "The Spindle is the safest place in all the cosmos, protected by the material of first creation, impenetrable even to the most petulant goddess."

"Hera," Lachesis explained, "is trying to enter the Spindle to return to Earth."

Clotho laughed. "That is her story, but it is not the real story."

"What is the real story?" I asked.

"I believe it is time." Lachesis looked over at Clotho, and then they both looked at me. "It is time to tell you the truth of the Spindle."

"I already know the truth," I scoffed. "You tell fortunes

and let souls back to Earth. Pretty simple, really. I've always wondered why so many tried so hard for so long to get inside."

"Because that is not the whole truth." Lachesis shook her head. "At best, it's a half-truth, shrouded in folklore, and told by people who did not know better." She paused and gave me a searching look. "The truth is much grander than any know, save for Hypnos, the fates, and Hera."

"What's the truth, then?" I asked.

"The spindle is not just a connection between the Fates and the Dream Realm, it is a connection between the Dream Realm and *Earth*."

"We alone protect the great nexus between the dreaming and the living," Lachesis added.

"Of course," I pointed behind me to the golden door that sent Rose back home. "Because of the door—"

"No," Clotho said. "The door is only a part of it. Buried deep below the Spindle, in the places only the dwarves may roam, past the core of the planet, there is a door that can only be opened by one of the fates. That door leads to Earth, and the other half of the Spindle, which can only be accessed at the top of the highest peak in the world, which we once called Mount Olympus."

"The gods cannot reach Earth by entering through the golden door," Lachesis said. "That is strictly for souls returning to their bodies. It is little more than a parlor trick. However, if the gods were to access the door at the core of the planet, then they could reenter the world and wreak havoc like the days of old."

I looked from one sister to the other. "Why are you telling me this now?"

"Because Hera is the reason we sealed off the door. She tried to get into the Spindle and use the door for herself.

She hired dwarves to dig into the core of the planet in hopes of finding the door. She will do anything to find it and return to Earth."

"You must find the door, Chelle." Lachesis's eyes were pleading.

"I must?" I asked, confused. "Why?"

"Because through that door is the core of the planet, the key to allowing dreamers back into Urgu and giving us a fighting chance for what is to come."

"What will I find in the core?"

"The Heart of Urgu, where all dreams enter the Dream Realm, and the center of all of our energy. It has been held fallow for one hundred years." Clotho was studying my face. "You must revive it, so that dreams may enter our realm again. You and you alone."

"Why me?"

"Because you have a body, and that is the most powerful thing in all of Urgu. No one else can bring the Dreamers back to this place. It is our only chance to stop what is to come."

"And Atropos knew this?"

Lachesis nodded. "She died because of it. Only a fate may open the door, and there can only be three. The fate who must save us all is you. If you do not find the core of the planet and revive it, then all of Urgu will fall into a thousand years of darkness."

I shook my head. "You've made a grave error in trusting me. I don't care about this place."

Clotho smiled. "Perhaps, but your paramour did."

"Rose," Lachesis said. "And if you bring back the Dreamers..."

"It will also bring her back," I said, breathlessly.

"Yes." Clotho smiled. "She will be able to visit this place again, in her dreams."

"That is a compelling case." I would do anything to see Rose again. "How? How do I do it?"

"It is an old spell. We will teach it to you," Lachesis said.

"Be careful though," Clotho added. "You will only have one opportunity to use it. It is powerful, old magic, reserved only for the Gods."

"Then how—?"

The Spindle rocked with another hit from Hera's forces, and it jolted me from the task at hand.

"That is a story for another time. Now, we must hurry," Clotho said, standing up with her sister. "Hera is angry, and in her anger, she is vulnerable."

"Are you sure the Spindle will hold?" I asked.

Clotho nodded. "It has held for a thousand generations and will do so for a thousand more, unless you fail. Whether we are here to guard it is the only thing that is unclear."

"Fine," I said. "I'm in."

"Come then," Lachesis said, grabbing my hand. "We have much work to do."

CHAPTER 7

AINE

The unrelenting shadow demons crashed upon the castle's exterior like tidal waves. Screams from the terrified citizens of the Emerald City echoed in the castle halls, but there was nothing we could do for those that remained outside. We had brought in those we could, but the shadow demons rushed through the city like a swarm of locusts, destroying everything in their path.

"No," I whispered to myself.

I watched the shadow demons from the throne room's balcony. The protections around the castle meant that no shadow demon could enter my sanctuary. Those that made it through the walls of the castle burnt up like comets, but that didn't stop them from smashing into the façade like fireballs and slamming into the windows like rocks.

"A pity, isn't it?" Hera's voice whispered as her purple eyes appeared on the balcony. "These poor citizens of yours had no idea that Nimue kept them so protected."

"You could stop this," I hissed.

Her eyes narrowed. "I could do a great many things, but why would I help those that betray me?"

"You believe I betrayed you?" I said, almost laughing.

"You betrayed her to whom I bestowed my blessing," Hera said. "Thus, you have betrayed me."

I scoffed. "I do not owe my loyalty to you, or any. I owe it to the Land of Oz."

"Please," Hera said, her voice booming. "Do not spin your logic on me, fairy. You are as materialistic and cold hearted as any who have served me. You wish to return to Earth and you will do anything to accomplish your goal."

I shrugged. "Why did I follow the Dreamer, then?"

"That's easy," Hera replied. "Because she was blessed by Hypnos, and you knew your best chance of getting back to Earth was with her. Now, it is with me."

"Please." I looked outside across the bridge. "Your shadow demons may have killed the hydra guarding it, but they cannot break through the Obsidian Spindle any easier than they can break into this castle."

Hera's glaring eyes moved forward until they nearly crossed the threshold of the castle. One more inch and the power of Hypnos's protection would singe her. "I did not expect you to care about the people in this city," she said in a low voice.

"Then I have a surprise for you because—"

"Don't care. Pontificating," Hera sighed. "I don't expect you to care about the people of Oz. However, I do think you care about your own dear Unseelie..." She trailed off, grinning maliciously.

I gasped. I hadn't thought about her forces moving through the Enchanted Woods. "Home," I muttered.

"Oh yes, your pink castle is quaint." Hera chuckled. "I dare even say it would be homey, though a little small for my taste."

My fists clenched at my sides. "I swear, if you destroyed the Enchanted Woods, I will—"

"You will what?" Hera asked. "You cannot even leave your castle to face me." She turned away. "However, you will be happy to know that I did not touch your precious forest, and your castle is quite intact, for now."

I knew I was defeated. "What do you want?"

"I want your help to open the Obsidian Spindle, so I can take what is mine."

"I can't do that. I have no way to open it, any more than you do. If I could—"

"You would, and you would leave everyone here to return to Earth. I know. That is why you are truly a creature of my own heart, and yet, I fear your heart is bigger than your mouth. And you have knowledge I need."

"I don't know what you're talking about."

"Where is the book?"

I cleared my throat, trying to maintain my composure. "Nimue took it."

"Where?" Hera asked. "I tire of this *tete-a-tete*."

"I don't know what Nimue did with it." That was a lie, but I didn't want to give away anything I could bargain away for clemency. "And I could not even read it if I did know."

Chelle had stolen the instruction manual for Urgu straight from the lair of Hera in the Dark Domain. Only one blessed by Hypnos could read the text inside its pages, so the book held little value for me.

"Don't tell me Nimue didn't rub it in your face."

I hadn't told anyone. However, after Chelle had taken Rose to the Spindle, I rushed back to her bed chamber to find the golden book. There, in the room, already holding it, was Nimue.

"Agree not to hurt me, and I will speak true."

"I agree," Hera said. "Interesting how in your people's hour of need, you think only of yourself."

I dropped my head. She was right.

"Speak now, fairy, and stay your forked tongue."

"I did see her," I said. "Only briefly."

"And what did she tell you?" Hera asked.

"She told me that she would once again gain the blessing of a god and return for her crown. And she plans to destroy you."

Nimue hadn't actually said anything about destroying Hera, but if I could put the god on her trail with a grudge, then perhaps Hera would leave the Emerald City and the Obsidian Spindle alone.

"And where did she say she was going? Don't act like she didn't tell you. She would gloat about her plans to anyone that listened. It was one of her most annoying qualities."

I chuckled. "She had many annoying qualities."

Hera laughed, too. "Tell me about it."

I looked up at her. "Swear to me that you will leave my people alone."

"Smart," Hera replied. "How much do I want this information?"

I looked into her dark purple eyes. "I bet you want it a lot."

"Fine," Hera's eyes narrowed. "I swear I will not hurt your fairies."

"No," I said. "All of Oz are my people now."

"That's rich." Hera chuckled. "You can't possibly believe that."

I puffed out my chest. "I am the Queen of Oz until Hypnos unseats me, or I am dusted. Say it."

Hera's eyes blinked slowly. "Nobody can compel me to say anything."

"Then, rot here," I said with a smile.

"This is exhausting," Hera sighed. "Very well, you are the queen, and should you help me, then I will not hurt any in Oz, assuming I get the book."

I nodded. "That is good enough for me." I fluttered through the vestibule and out onto the balcony. "Call off your dogs."

Hera snapped her fingers, and the shadow demons hovered in place. "That is enough." They floated toward the sky and hovered there, like a shroud of fog over the city. "Everyone will be fine until I return and release them back to the Dark Domain."

I nodded. "Then follow me."

I felt a cold hand on my shoulder. Closing my eyes, I vanished, hoping I had made the right decision. I was always good at hitching my fate to the most powerful person in the room, and none in all of Oz was as powerful as Hera.

CHAPTER 8

ROSE

I sat in the dining hall of the campus cafeteria, watching the kitchen staff churn out meal after meal. I couldn't afford one, but I loved to watch them work. In another life, I would have been a chef. Of course, in another life, I was also a queen. That life was stolen from me, and I was left with nothing except the memories of my power and my yearning to be back in the Dream Realm.

I held my fingers under the table, and whispered spells to them under my breath. "Ignite. Fire. *Lux.*" I'd tried all number of words since I woke up, but no matter what I said, there was no magic left in me.

Across the cafeteria, I watched a bright-eyed Jamil walk over to me. She smiled and waved as she carried her lunch tray with her. She might have been able to buy lunch but didn't make enough money to afford a place on campus, so she took to squatting in the parking lot with the rest of the vagrant. That was how we met.

"Hey, Rose," Jamil said, sliding in across from me. "I haven't seen you around much since—well, you know. I was starting to think you were avoiding me."

I was.

"No, I wasn't." The lie would have once meant something to me, made me uncomfortable. I valued honesty. But now, nothing mattered. "I was just...it's hard to be so far away. I have to drive down every day, now that—"

"Yeah, I heard that you lost the van. It's a shame. Chelle's gonna be pissed."

"She's not here anymore, Jamil. She's—" It felt stupid to say it out loud. Jamil was a wood nymph, and thus she understood magic, but the rest of the people around me would have thought me crazy if I talked about the Dream Realm in the open. I kept my mouth shut in public.

"I know where she is," Jamil replied, sensing my hesitation.

My eyes dropped. "She's not coming back."

Jamil shook her head. "Don't say that. After all, you did, and she can, too."

"I...I don't know if I want her to." I caught her eyes, and then we both turned away. "She knew I didn't want to be back here. She knew it. And yet, here I am. How could she...?"

Jamil placed her hand on mine. "I'm sure she had her reasons."

I cringed and pulled away from her. "I don't know. The last thing I remember was getting a crown placed on my head, and then I wound up here. It was good. I was good. I remember joy in my heart."

"That sucks." Jamil cut her sandwich in two and took a bite of one half, and then pushed the tray over toward me. "Here. You must be hungry."

"I don't need your pity," I said to her.

"Yes, you do." She gave a slight smile. "But this isn't pity. It's friendship."

I barely waited for her to finish her sentence before I inhaled the other half of her sandwich and a handful of chips. "Fine. You're right. I do."

"I know."

I swallowed my food, and then took a deep breath. "Since we're friends, I need to ask you something else."

"Anything," Jamil said.

"I need you to help me get back to—" I looked around, and then leaned in. "You know where."

Jamil's eyebrows shot up and she shook her head. "No. Anything but that. I already lost one friend to that crappy place, and I almost lost you as well, I can't—"

"You helped Chelle," I said, stony-eyed. "Why won't you help me?"

She tore into her sandwich and spoke with her mouth full. "She was going there to save you."

"And I'm going back to save her."

"You know that's not true. You're going there to save yourself." Jamil bit her lip.

"So what if I am?" I said, my mouth full of chips. "I can do two things. I am very nuanced."

Jamil shook her head. "It's a bad idea."

I stared at her for a long time in silence. "Does that mean you won't help me?"

She nodded. "I already said I wouldn't."

"I'm going back, Jamil. With you or without you."

"That sounds ominous."

"It's not. It's a fact." I stuck my finger down on the table to make a point, then leaned forward so only Jamil could hear me. "I already have a bottle of pills, and if that doesn't work, then I can stop taking my insulin."

Jamil pushed back from the table. "So, it's suicide, then."

"Shut up! Not so loud." I stared at her, my jaw clenched. "And not if you help me."

Jamil sighed. "That's a hell of a thing to ask."

"I know, and I know I'm a bitch...I just...don't care."

She glared at me. "That really makes you a queen bitch, then."

"I was a queen," I said bitterly. "And now I'm a bitch, too. But come on, you kind of care about me, which means you don't want me to die trying something stupid."

Jamil sighed. "This is all stupid, but fine. I'll help you."

I smiled at her. "Thank you."

"Don't thank me." She swallowed the last of her sandwich. "You know what you're getting into."

CHAPTER 9
RED

I did not enjoy the sea. I was made for solid ground and the sea, even one made of sand, tied my stomach in knots. I liked a place where I could plant my legs and maintain my balance.

"How much further, mage?" I asked the ram-horned wizard guiding our ship.

"Unclear," he said without taking his eyes from the sandy waves. "The sand shifts under our feet all the time. I follow the tallest mountain, and as long as it points across my bow, then I am headed in the right way."

"That is Agrona's mountain," Boudica added, looking off into the distance at a tall mountain surrounded by a halo of black clouds.

"True," the wizard said. "But we are not journeying there. Or at least I am not. We are simply using it as a reference point. It's all very safe, I assure you."

"That does not make me rest easy. I would not wish to go to that mountain should it be the last place on Earth," Boudica mumbled, turning away.

"Why?" I asked, walking toward her. "It was your home."

"The Mountains are my home, but Agrona is not my god. She turned her back on us, and I turned my back on her. Her people wept for her help, and she stayed in her castle, locked away, unwilling to help us."

I placed a hand on Boudica's broad shoulder. "But you helped yourself. That is what matters."

"Aye," she said, looking at me. Her fiery eyes glowed with burning rage. "We did, and I have no desire to go back there."

"We won't," I said.

"That's not entirely true," said the wizard from the front of the boat. "If you seek the Cave of Wonder, you may return to Agrona's kingdom yet. Some legends say the cave is in the Mountains."

"Aye, I have heard the same legends," Boudica said. "And ones that place it on the furthest reaches of the Sandlands, and those that would send me to the Bogs, or the Mistreach. I would prefer any to the Mountains."

"As you should." The wizard turned his boat to the right. "If you go to the Mountains, you will find the war."

"What war?" I asked.

"The war to end all wars. The forces of the Sandlands are fighting the horrible monsters from the Mountains. Sekhmet's army is fierce, but as you know, warrior, the creatures that roam the Mountains are ferocious. Even infusing her soldiers with her will is barely enough to keep the monsters at bay, and more come every day."

"Ferocious, and bound to the Mountain Realm until recently," Boudica replied.

I frowned. "They have always been solitary creatures."

"Maybe once, but they amassed and came for us in the

Sandlands. They cannot get over the Wall of Itherium due to Hypnos's magic, but they can invade the rest of Urgu, and the Sandlands is the gateway to a great many places."

The boat rose over a great sand dune, and slammed back down, creaking and rocking violently. Mounds of sand piled onto the deck and stung my eyes. The smell of the acrid sea filled my nostrils, and I had to spit it out of my mouth.

"I hate the sand."

"And it hates you, I have been told," Boudica replied.

Before I could laugh, the wizard scoffed. "The sand hates everyone. Urgu hates us all, and it will swallow us all up, given enough time."

Cheery.

Another great crash against the boat jostled us out of our seats. This was not from the sea itself, I realized. Something was ramming us. Another crash upon us, and then another.

"Hold on!" the wizard shouted, fear gripping his tongue.

"What's happening?" I screamed.

"I don't—Oh my god."

I turned to see what he was staring at, mouth agape, and my mouth fell open, too. A massive tentacle crested over the bow of the ship and slammed onto the deck. The thing was black, with green suckers running down each of its enormous tentacles. I dove to avoid its reach and grabbed Boudica, pulling her toward the stern as another tentacle wrapped around the ship.

Boudica's eyes flashed when she finally caught a glimpse of it. "That beast is from the Mountains," she gasped, rushing toward the back of the ship. The tentacles squeezed the helm and the wood cracked under the great pressure. "A hideous creature that is voraciously hungry."

"BACK!" The wizard shouted. "*Volida!*" A giant fireball appeared in his hands and he flung it at the tentacles.

Boudica drew her broadsword from behind her back and rushed the monster as it cracked the bow of the ship in half. "We must save the ship!"

But it was too late to save anything. As she rushed forward, the great monster lifted the ship into the air and slammed it back down onto the sand. With a great crunching sound, the ship snapped in half and I was flung overboard into the unforgiving sand.

I struggled to reach the surface as the sand worked to pull me under for good. Finally, with the last of my strength, I broke through and took a deep, grateful breath of air. The monster was nowhere to be found. Only the wreckage of the ship gave any indication that the beast had been there at all. I grabbed onto the nearest piece of wood and pulled myself up.

"Boudica!" I shouted but got no response. I picked up another piece of floating wreckage and used it like an oar to paddle through the thick sand. "Boudica!"

"HERE!" I heard her shout back from somewhere in the distance. I moved toward the sound until I caught sight of her. Boudica bobbed in the sea, struggling to stay above the crashing sand.

I grabbed her hand and pulled her onto my floating piece of wood, but we only succeeded in dragging my wreckage under the sea with her. I looked around desperately. There, just ahead of us, was a mangled lifeboat. I used my arms to swim through the sandy sea and with Boudica's help managed to right the boat and dive inside. We lay there, heaving, for a long time.

"What do we do now?" Boudica finally asked when we'd caught our breath.

I lifted my head from the floor and looked around until I saw Agrona's mountain. "Now, we make for the mountain. Better hope the wizard was right that we'll find land along the way."

I pulled a piece of wood out of the wreckage and used it to paddle through the unforgiving sea. Boudica followed suit, and together we hoped to find land.

NIMUE

"How much longer until we reach Epiales?" I asked the invisible monster. I was already sick of the Nightmare Realm's black and neon aesthetic. At least Urgu had light, real light, and not whatever the stuff was in this new place.

"It's much further. Epiales rests in the deepest corner of the Nightmare Realm. We will make it, if you follow me closely. Do not venture off the path."

Trails of neon lit the ground like stars in the sky. It was beautiful and surreal at once. Only the haunted breathing sounds brought me back to the horrible reality of this place; the screams echoing through the wind sent chills down my spine.

"I hate this place."

The mouth laughed. "That is because it was not meant for you. It was meant for me and my kin. We filled it with that which we loved, and then, you humans invaded it until there were more of you than us."

"Then why don't I see any?"

The teeth turned toward me, and grinned. "Because they are delicious."

"I do not believe you," I replied, nonplussed. "Souls are nothing but dust when they are destroyed, and I doubt you care much for dust."

The beast scoffed. "For someone who knows so little about souls, you have such an air of arrogance about you."

"Then please, enlighten me."

"You should be grateful it is so dark to your eyes. Otherwise, you would go insane. Of course, to me who grew out of the darkness, this place is beautiful and horrible at once."

Something crunched under my foot. "I understand how it could be horrible."

"I understand, and I sympathize, but you chose to come here. I think you should accept the madness and lean into it."

"I'll take it under advisement," I said with a grunt.

"Do so," the teeth vanished from sight, and suddenly I was alone in the darkness. "Or I will leave you to rot."

The growling from every side grew louder and the hot breath of the beasts closed in on me. The neon spots surrounded me, and I gulped loudly, my eyes darting wildly for something familiar, something safe.

"No, please. I do not want that," I said. "I will endeavor to be...more accepting in the future."

The teeth came back into sight, and the neon moved back into the night. "Very well. You learn quickly."

"Why do they listen to you?" I asked.

"They fear me, as all should in this place. Even here, I am the nightmare. I was here when Epiales was new to this world. He brought me from Earth, as his eternal pet."

"His pet?"

"I was always a true pet," he said, with melancholy in his voice. "Always true." He was silent for a moment, and the only sound was the guttural breathing of monsters out there in the darkness. "Now come, there is nothing to fear except the fear of everything around you."

In the distance, a figure loomed atop a ledge. A shadow hung in the light that surrounded it. As we closed in, an eerie dread filled my stomach. The mouth moved toward it, even as the thing grew more haunting.

"What is that?"

"The lady," the mouth said.

I groaned. "You didn't say anything about a lady."

"All travelers lost in the darkness will find the lady eventually, and she will help guide you into the next phase of your journey."

"I thought you were taking me?"

"And you believed me, even when you said you wouldn't." The beast laughed. "That was just something I said to get you to follow me. First step, honey. Don't trust anyone in the Nightmare Realm. Except the Lady, who is very kind to stragglers."

"Said the liar," I said. "I think I just won't trust anyone."

"You learn quickly," the mouth smiled. "Perhaps you will not die after all."

"She's going to eat me, isn't she?"

"Not unless you give her a reason to. Of course, why would you believe me?" The teeth hovered toward the vision in the darkness. "My lady, I bring one who has been lost in the wilderness. She seeks council with Epiales, and she has powers which might aid you in your quest."

As I neared, I noticed the woman stood not on legs, but on a scaly tail like a serpent. She rose high into the air and a hiss escaped from her. It did not come from her mouth, but from the snakes on her head. They snapped at the air, their red eyes glowing at me.

Why does it always have to be Gorgons?

She slithered closer and studied me. "What manner of reason come you to the Realm of Nightmares, child?"

"Child?" I grimaced. "I'm hundreds of years old."

"And yet, only a child in this place. Answer me or be left to the darkness."

I chose to tell the truth, which might have been a mistake in a place like this, filled with lies and deception. "I come from the Dream Realm, at the behest of Agrona, to find the Nightmare God Epiales, free him, and tell him that his love waits for him."

"Epiales does not care about this place, or any other. There is no love in him."

I stepped forward. "Then I will tell him, and he will not care. But I will find him, then find a way out of the Nightmare Realm back to Earth."

The Gorgon laughed. "That is quite the delusion, even for this place."

The mouth joined in the chorus of laughter.

"I'm not here to be insulted." I crossed my arms. "Can you help me or not?"

"That depends. Can you help me?" The Gorgon turned to the smiling teeth. "You say she has powers?"

"She does," the mouth replied, turning to me. "Show her."

I nodded. "Light." From my hands, light glowed slowly. "There is much more."

"Interesting," the Gorgon replied. "Very well. A test, then. If you pass, I shall help you reach Epiales. If you fail, then you will be dusted, no matter."

"How do I know I can trust you?" I asked.

"You must not trust anyone. Not in this place."

"At least you are honest," I said. "But I reject your offer."

The Gorgon slithered even closer to me, smiling. "Then you will be left for dead. I have no use for you."

I pointed to the invisible beast. "I can just use my new friend here to find Epiales."

She smiled even wider. "The only reason he has not killed you is because I pay him to bring all travelers to me." The Gorgon pulled three black pebbles from her purse around her waist and held them out. The teeth manifested into a purple, feline creature with bright green eyes. He nodded and placed the pebbles into a satchel around his chest.

"Our bargain is reached. Pleasure doing business with you." With that, the cat creature turned to me with a grin. "It would have been so much nicer to eat you, my dear, but I suppose you will be spared for another time." The cat vanished into the night, his mouth the last part of him to disappear.

"Come with me if you value your life," the Gorgon said. I had no choice but to believe her. Whatever lived in the darkness was too dangerous for me to fight alone, and she was the only sanctuary afforded me in this cold, cruel place. I already knew death lay in the darkness, and I had no interest in dying in such a dreadful place. At least with the Lady, I knew what evil I faced.

CHAPTER II

AINE

Hera and I stood outside of Agrona's castle, the Emerald City now miles away, even though we'd only traveled for an instant. While I had never been to the mountain castle before, I had always felt its power in Urgu, looming in the distance, ever since Hypnos had disappeared. It was growing stronger now. The castle was built into the highest peak in the Mountain Realm, and from it, you could see hundreds of miles into the distance.

Or you could, if the entire top of the mountain wasn't covered in a thick layer of black smoke and clouds. It smelled like a foot and looked even worse. The entrance to the castle wasn't a proper door but resembled the mouth of a hideous monster. When I pushed on the door, goop stuck to my hand, and a large tongue rolled out to greet us.

"Be prepared for anything," Hera said as she stepped onto the tongue and made her way into the castle, but she didn't have to tell me. I was already prepared for the horrific. I lived in the Dream Realm. I was built for horrific.

I unfurled my wings and fluttered into the castle. We didn't get far before lightning electrified the hallway and a boom of thunder quaked through it. The black walls were lit with blue light, and I stopped to gather my nerves after another crackle of thunder and flash of lightning barreled toward us from the other end of the hallway. Hera walked slowly but confidently, and I fluttered behind her, unmoored by how quickly I lost my nerve.

"Agrona!" Hera shouted as she made her way down the hallway. "I come to parlay with you."

"Go away!" a shrill voice said from the end of the hall. "I don't parlay with the worthless."

The hallway broke into a large throne room. Against the wall on the left of us, spanning the length and height of the gigantic room, a huge blue portal crackled and spun. Across from it, a woman sat on a tall throne made of black bone. Her eyes shone with bright, white light that matched her hair. She was draped in furs as she sat regally, unencumbered by the weight of her position.

Hera stared, mouth agape, at the spinning portal. "What have you done?"

"What you couldn't, sister," Agrona said, dryly. "While you worked to manipulate humans into opening the Spindle, I found a way through the veil and into the Nightmare Realm."

"The Nightmare Realm?" Hera said. "Epiales wouldn't—"

Agrona slammed her hands down. "My love would do anything for me. Together, we will lay waste to the Dream Realm, and he will rule this place. In return, he will let me back to Earth to have my revenge against the gods who slighted me."

"Why didn't you tell me?" Hera said. "I could have helped."

"Helped!" Agrona said, standing. "I do not need your help. I never needed your help. You are weak."

As she rose, I glimpsed something shining beneath her. I flew higher into the air and realized the glimmer came from the golden book that Hera kept, the theft of which was the reason for our visit to Agrona's castle.

"There it is!" I shouted. "On the throne."

"That was easy," Hera smirked. "Give that book to me, Agrona."

Agrona's blazing eyes landed on me. "You have chosen your side, little one. I shall remember that." She stepped down from her throne. She was taller than Hera, and broader, and I got the sudden feeling that I made a grave mistake.

"We do not have to do this, Agrona," Hera said.

"Why not?" Agrona replied. "I am the superior fighter and have no fear of you. If anything, you should beg for your life."

Hera flicked her wrist and two strands of shadow bound Agrona's wrists. The shadows broke apart when Agrona flexed her arms.

"Fool." Agrona bent to the ground, anchoring herself there as tendrils of light sparked in her eyes and shot out toward Hera.

I lost track of Hera in the sparks. I fluttered over toward the throne and hid behind the dark bone, hoping it would protect me from any stray magic that erupted between them.

"I control the light now, Hera!" Agrona hugged herself, and then flung her arms outward. A blinding light exploded from her chest and filled the room. I had to squeeze my eyes shut against its brilliance. There was a scream.

I opened my eyes to see Agrona holding Hera up by her

hair. She looked less like a queen and more like a sniveling bug, her long legs kicking from under her black dress, and her black hair bound up in Agrona's bony fingers. I had never seen Hera struggle before.

"Let me go!" Hera demanded. Even in defeat, she would not beg.

"I would have come for you eventually. My love would not allow any god to survive his wrath. You will die now, and Sehkmet next. Then, we will come for Anansi and Loki. All will bow to Epiales and then, I will have revenge."

"Hypnos won't allow it," Hera said. "He will stop you."

"He is weak and feeble and has been cast out from this place."

Hera gasped for air, still clawing against Agrona. "He will return, and he will take his revenge on you."

"Maybe," Agrona replied with a wry smile. "But you will not be around to see it."

"I wi—" Hera began, but her breath left her. Agrona placed her hand on Hera's chest, and a burst of light broke the purple-eyed goddess into a million pieces.

She was dead.

Hera was the most powerful being I had ever laid eyes on. I believed she rivaled Hypnos's power even in Urgu. Out in the universe, away from his realm, he would have been putty in Hera's hands.

Agrona had killed a god, and she would not stop at one. If she could do that to Hera, she could destroy anyone or anything, and she had her eyes out for me. I had to find the other gods and hope that at least one would listen to me. Only together could they fight Agrona. She was too powerful for any one of them alone.

Everything in me was bent on escaping, but I remembered the golden book and snatched it up. The gods had no reason to entreat with me. If I brought the book to them, they would have to take me seriously.

"Leave that be!" Agrona shouted, turning to me.

She reached out her arm. Lightning built up in her palm, but before she could zap me, I disappeared into the ether. I had to warn my people. I had left them for dead with their fight against Hera and the shadow demons, but I could not let them fight the burden of Agrona's wrath without at least a warning. I had to tell them that doom was coming for them.

CHAPTER 12

ROSE

The dorm smelled acrid and sickly sweet in a swirling combination that assaulted my nostrils and stuck to my tongue. It was nothing like the standard musty odor college residences I had entered in my time at school, but quite unpleasant in its own right.

"I really don't want to do this," Jamil said as we rounded a pristine hallway. It looked as if no one had walked through it in months.

The floor gleamed with my reflection and I stared down at it, startled for a moment. Once I had life in me, but I didn't recognize the girl who looked back at me now. All her color, all her life had drained away. "I don't care." It was true. I didn't care about anything, not even a little bit, and hadn't since I came back from the Dream Realm. Yes, I wanted to return there, but I couldn't explain to Jamil that the true reason was because I hoped it would help me feel something again, even if it was the pain of Chelle's betrayal.

"I know," Jamil said with a sigh. "This is a really bad idea though, and I have to keep harping on it."

I shrugged. "You do what you have to do, as long as it ends with you helping me."

"I'm helping. I'm helping!" Jamil said with a huff. "You know, I liked you better before you became a dick."

"Me too." I don't know who the person was that came back from Urgu, but it didn't feel like me. I had my memories, but they didn't feel real. It was like I was simply a facsimile of myself. I could remember the idea of being happy, or sad, or even angry, but I couldn't remember the feeling itself. I was an alien looking back at a life I didn't understand, even though I had been the one who lived it.

Jamil stopped at a door in the middle of the hallway. It was plain, no different than any other, with no flair or indication that it could lead me back to the Dream Realm. "Whatever you do, don't look Teddy in the eyes," she said before knocking vigorously.

"Go away!" A thickly-accented male voice shouted from the other side of the door. "I'm busy!"

"I don't care!" Jamil yelled back. "I have another lost soul for you."

"I'm at capacity with lost souls right now. Come back later."

"No! Get your ass out here, Teddy. There is no way I can deal with this one by myself for another minute. Either you murder her, or I will."

"Hey!" I pinched Jamil on the arm. "That's not nice."

"Well, you are not nice," Jamil said. "You change and so will my opinion."

I was trying. I really was, but I needed to get back into the Dream Realm. Jamil was the only person who could help me so I was leaning on her harder than I should have. I knew that, I just wasn't capable of doing anything about it.

"She sounds cute," Teddy said from the other side of the door. "Is she cute?"

Jamil eyed me up and down. "She's pretty, in a waify sort of way."

"I love waify." Skittering sounds behind the door preceded the jiggle of the door handle. A pale white man with sunken cheeks and fiery hair pressed himself against the doorjamb, staring out from behind thick sunglasses. "Why, hello there."

"Hi," I replied, taking a small step back. He had a creepy vibe about him, like he would just as quickly slice my throat as kiss it.

"My," he replied. "You are *waify*." He let the last word linger on his tongue, which he flicked when he was done speaking. It was one of the least attractive things I had ever seen.

"Thank...you?"

"Just like I said," Jamil replied. "Can we come in or not? This empty hallway is creeping me out."

Teddy clicked his tongue. "You're the only person I know who is more creeped out by the hallway than what's inside."

Jamil rolled her eyes. "I've been dealing with vampires for years, and they're more gothy melodrama than anything. 'Oh, poor me, the world is so hard and mean.' There is nothing scary about that. It's just pathetic."

"...ouch," Teddy said with a playful smile. He moved aside so that we could enter.

I didn't want to be in the room. I flattened myself against the wall once I entered. "You're a vampire?"

"What's it to you, love?" Teddy's sly grin revealed a set of fanged canines. He licked one of them slowly, as if it was supposed to turn me on. It didn't. It wouldn't have turned me on even if I was straight or had the capacity to feel. "Does it scare you?" he asked.

I shook my head. "No. I used to date a Gorgon. Just about nothing scares me."

"A Gorgon! I know one of those."

"Yeah," Jamil said, nodding. "This is her girlfriend."

Teddy let out a thin, high-pitched laugh. "Wow, Jamil. Another one? You trying to get me to collect the whole set?"

Jamil shook her head. "Chelle went into the Dream Realm for this girl, and she made it, Teddy. She really made it."

Teddy placed his hands on his hips. "Well I'll be dipped."

"Yeah, I know. Crazy, right?" Jamil said, wide-eyed and excited for a moment, before taking a breath and mellowing herself. "And this one got back out, which is even crazier. It's a miracle, but this dummy wants to go back in, which makes her the stupidest person I know."

"Ungrateful," Teddy said, cocking his head as he studied me. "Rude."

A moan came from the open door of what appeared to be a bedroom. "Come back to bed, baby."

Teddy spoke over his shoulder without taking his eyes off of me. "Be back in a minute, love."

"Sorry," I said. "Are you busy?"

"Always, darling, but no more than normal." Teddy looked back at his bedroom, then, nonplussed, turned to us. "Maybe less so, actually. Come on in. Let's get this over with."

The only light in Teddy's room came from the black bulb hanging from the ceiling. The posters on the walls glowed green and depicted monsters, skeletons, and cats with devilish looks on their faces. A man no older than me laid naked on the bed. He was thin as a rail, and his arms and neck held multiple puncture wounds.

"Jesus Christ!" I breathed. "What are you doing to that poor boy!"

"Boy?" the man said. His lip curled. "Rude."

"She is quite rude, love," Teddy replied, then turned back to me. "I'm not doing anything this sweet thing doesn't want, I promise you that."

"It's true, Daddy," the man moaned. "Come on, we weren't finished."

"See? Nothing untoward." Teddy dragged his finger across his lover's lips. "Consent is the cornerstone to BDSM. We don't have to hunt anymore, baby. The willing come right to us."

"Gross," Jamil said. "But not grosser than anything else I've seen."

"Quite," Teddy said. "We are all really gross. So, how can I help you?"

"You're the only person I know who even cares about the Dream Realm, so I'm hoping you can dissuade my friend from going back."

I scoffed. "I am going back. If your aim is to stop me, then you're barking up the wrong tree."

"You ain't going back with that jacked-up soul, honey," the man in Teddy's bed said, propping himself on his elbows.

"Excuse me?" I replied.

He circled his arm around himself and snapped his fingers in an overly-flamboyant motion. "Your soul is all jacked up. I've never seen one broken into so many pieces."

"Sorry about him," Teddy said. "Hiram can sense people's auras. That's how we met, actually. He guessed I was an old soul, just not quite how old." He pinched Hiram as he said this, and the two of them giggled.

"I can see your soul, girl," Hiram said to me. "Or at least what's left of it. It's been broken into a million little pieces. Your soul is barely holding together right now. It's just your body keeping it from flittering off into space."

It hit me like a flood. *He was right.*

I remembered everything about my coronation—my assassination. I was stabbed in the back, literally, in the Dream Realm. At my coronation. Edwina...the priest. She—she stabbed me! Aine, Red...Chelle...they tried to save me. Chelle...she didn't force me home...she somehow got me home to save me.

She didn't betray me.

She loved me.

The slightest smile rose across my face. I felt the littlest of butterflies flitter through my stomach. It was happiness, I thought. Happiness because Chelle didn't betray me. She saved me, somehow. Even as that happiness faded again, and I was just as dead inside as before, I was filled with even more resolution to return to Urgu and find Chelle.

"Guys, I have to get back. Chelle...I need Chelle."

"You ain't getting back to the Dream Realm with your swiss-cheese-ass soul," Hiram said.

"What do you know about it?" I replied.

Hiram scoffed. "I know that the Dream Realm is full of *souls,* and if you don't have a complete soul, you aren't going to get back there."

I placed my hands on my hips. "My girlfriend made it inside with her body, I can, too."

"Nuh-uh."

"Enough!" Jamil said. "You're giving me a headache. How do we fix it, Hiram?"

Hiram shrugged his boyish shoulders. "How should I know? That's way over my skill level. I just see 'em. I don't fix them. You gotta figure out how to mold your soul back together." He flicked his wrists. "These hands don't fix anything."

"Well, what can I do?" I asked.

Hiram thought for a minute. "Only a really powerful demon or a god can do that kind of magic, and the most powerful being I know is Teddy."

"Thank you, my love," Teddy said with a smile. When he turned back to Jamil, his face dropped "I'm afraid if you need a demon...you know where you have to go."

"Don't say it," Jamil replied.

"What?" I said, confused.

"We have to go to Sacramento," Jamil said with a sigh.

"Bingo," Teddy said, slipping back into bed. "Now, please leave. I have business to attend."

"Yes, Daddy," Hiram replied, melting into Teddy's arms. I left, not wanting to see the next part, but fearing it was already implanted in my brain forever.

CHAPTER 13
NIMUE

My new Gorgon chaperone led me through the neon darkness without incident until we reached the tip of a hill, where neon fruits grew from the bushes. Underneath us, down a rocky ridge, laid an intricate web, lit somehow by an unknown source.

The longer I stayed in the Nightmare Realm, the less I understood it. The darkness felt oppressive but there, my mind could at least wander toward happier times. I found myself hating the light, where beasts snuck around in the shadows just out of eyesight. That, more than anything, sent my mind into the most awful places.

"What are we doing here?" I asked the Gorgon as she crept toward the edge of the ridge.

"I need to be sure I can trust you," she said. "And there is no better test than combat. Several Dreamers are caught in the web of Nefeski, the cruelest beast in the Schrylands."

"Dreamers?" I asked, confused. "There are Dreamers here?"

She nodded. "Not like the ones in the Dream Realm, but yes. Those stuck here are doomed to a life of chaos until they are eaten or killed in some grotesque manner. Usually they die before I can reach them. Here, we are in luck because Nefeski keeps her prey for months, waiting for the perfect time to eat them.”

“It sounds like a stupid idea to save them,” I replied. “We should just let them die.”

The Gorgon shook her head. “It is not their fault they ended up here. In better times, they might have been able to survive and make it to the Dream Realm, but a great evil has taken hold here. The creatures of the night are gaining strength. Without our help, all human souls in the realm will die.”

“Well, good, honestly. Better dead than stuck here.”

“Interesting perspective, though misguided.” The Gorgon rose to the tip of her tail. “You are not completely wrong, but people can still make a life here, though admittedly a difficult one. I hope to bring them to safety and give them a chance, even in this place. At least as good a chance as I can muster. I take them to a camp not far from here where they can hope for a semblance of normalcy. I’ll take you there, too.”

“I have no interest in staying any longer than I must,” I replied, standing with her. “I intend to find Epiales and then make my way to Earth as quickly as possible.”

The Gorgon nodded. “It is a good plan. However, I have seen others lost in the Nightmare Realm for centuries until the madness overtakes them and they become the monsters they once feared.”

“Is that even possible?” I asked.

“Anything is possible here,” the Gorgon replied. “I have seen worse than a human soul transforming into a monstrous one.”

I looked down at my hands, already wasting away into

nothing from using a few bits of magic. "Well, I don't have an eternity. I have thirty days. Less, now."

"Then you will need help, and I will give it to you. There is one who can give us what we need to find the Nightmare King, but his price is not cheap."

I sighed. "Let me guess. It's in that web."

"Very good. My contact desires the egg of a spider," the Gorgon replied. "That is the price. If you help me, I will secure one of the eggs, and we will see the one who can help you."

I grumbled. "Fine. Despite my better nature being predicated on *not* sticking my neck out for anyone, I will help you if it furthers my aim."

"Splendid," the Gorgon said. "Then we will away." She slid down the rock path until she reached the bottom. In the dark I couldn't see where the hill began or ended, so I stumbled until my foot lurched to a stop at the bottom and I rolled along the ground.

The web itself was massive. One strand of the webbing was thicker than my arm, each link in the intricate pattern nearly as long as my torso. I looked up to see the source of the web's light—it was created by a hive of what looked like a combination of iridescent bees, spiders, and butterflies. Their nest hovered at the top of the web, trapped by Nefeski's sticky goo. Beneath that, a sack of oval, glowing green rocks pulsated in time with the fluttering of the butterfly wings.

"Nefeski's eggs require heat to open, and there is little of it here."

I had felt the chill in the air since I entered the Nightmare Realm, but it was only when the Gorgon mentioned it that I became aware of the frigid air running through my body. I had thought that the cold came from the fear coursing through my veins, but it was more than that.

"Look," the Gorgon said, pointing to heaving balls of webbing speckled throughout the web. "Those are Dreamers. Help them break free, and I will secure an egg from Nefeski's sac."

"That sounds dangerous," I said.

"Extremely." The Gorgon pushed off from the ground and closed her eyes. "Smooth as silk and slippery as butter."

She clasped her hands together, and as she reared up onto the tip of her tail, her body began to glow a dark red. A spell. She had magic, which could prove helpful on my quest for Epiales. Perhaps our meeting would not be a complete waste of time.

"Now you," she said.

I shook my head. She knew I had magic as well, but what she didn't know was that every time I used my magic, I weakened a little bit. "It's your spell, so you do it to me."

"Fine, but you will have to use it on the other Dreamers," she replied, holding her hands out to me. "Smooth as silk and slippery as butter."

I looked down at my hands, which started to glow a dark red pulsating in time with her light. I placed my hand on the spider web, and instead of getting stuck, I could release my hand with ease.

"Wonderful."

"Thank you for trusting me," the Gorgon said. "This is the first step."

"Don't try to bond with me." I hoisted myself up onto the web. "We're still about to do the dumbest thing I can imagine."

The Gorgon slid onto the spider web. "Fair enough." She

slithered toward the egg sac at the top of the web, and I continued on to the first of five wriggling Dreamers.

What spell could I use that wouldn't drain my energy too much and still free them? I ran across the spindly web and knelt in front of the first wriggling bundle. "Don't move. I'm here to help you." I placed my hand in the air and whispered, "Fire."

Flames rose in my hand, and I pressed them down to the trapped human. The webbing sizzled and then loosened enough for me to pull it apart. A middle-aged woman emerged, staring at me with horrified blue eyes.

"What happ—"

"Shhh—" I said. "This is a nightmare, and we have to get you out of this place right now." I pointed down to the ground. "Meet me there, and don't run. You won't like what you find in the darkness. Do you understand?"

She nodded.

I performed the gorgon's anti-stickiness spell on the girl. The use of magic caused a pang in my side, but I had to keep going. My soul would break apart soon enough without the blessing from Epiales, so I needed to find him quickly. I released the second and third bundles, finding a child no older than ten and an old man. Once they were safe at the bottom of the cliff, I turned to the fourth, and that is when I saw the Gorgon hard charging me.

"Run!" she shouted. As she passed me, I saw that under her arm she held one of the glowing green eggs from the sac. I heard a foul scream. The entire web shook at once, bouncing me high into the air. The Gorgon snatched me out of the air and pulled me onto her back.

"What's happening?" I screamed.

"She has woken up," the Gorgon replied. "And she is not

happy we are messing with her dinner and stealing her children."

Eight legs skittered toward me, and a thousand eyes came into view, glowing with an evil, haunting green. Her pincers opened and another great scream shook the web.

"Fire!" I shouted, and my hands went up in flames. I conjured a huge stream of fire that set the web ablaze. "Lightning!"

Lightning bolts shot from my hands toward the spider, who reared up into the air and slammed back down onto the web. The web tendrils buckled and snapped under us just as we reached the end of the web, and the Gorgon slithered off toward the group of humans. They screamed in unison at her appearance.

"Get on!" she screamed, but the humans stood shocked at her, unable to move.

"Get on!" I shouted. "Or take your chances with the spider." I looked back to see Nefeski howling through the flames as she worked her way toward us. "And she's going to be quite irate when she reaches us."

The humans didn't wait another second. They snapped out of their trance and rushed onto the Gorgon's back. She slithered forward with the spider egg under her arm. I was one step closer to Epiales.

CHAPTER 14
CHELLE

"No, no, no," Lachesis said, disgusted. She was watching me perform the same spell incorrectly for the hundredth time. "You're still saying it wrong. This is old magic, very unforgiving. It would kill you as soon as help you, so you must be more careful, more precise."

She had been trying to teach me the spell for three days. Every time I tried to replicate her words, I did it wrong, and every time I fixed the pronunciation, some other imperfection showed up in my phrasing.

"Then you do it," I grumbled.

"I already told you that neither Clotho nor I can restart the Heart of Urgu, because neither of us have bodies, which means we do not have the requisite power—"

I pressed my fingers into the sides of my nose. "You know, it's pretty stupid that the ONLY thing that can restart the Heart of Urgu and allow Dreamers to come back to Urgu is the one thing nobody in Urgu has except me: a body."

Lachesis shrugged. "You say that it is stupid, but I say it is mighty convenient that you came at our time of greatest need."

I held up a shaky finger. "That is ONE way to look at it, but an insanely stupid way."

Lachesis smiled smugly. "Says you."

I nodded. "Yes, that is accurate. I do say that."

"Try again and enunciate this time. You sound like you have a bag of marbles in your mouth."

The oldest magic dated back before the written word and was more a series of grunts than an attempt at real language. "*Uhrt Elostrnt Rtincyru.*"

"Close," Lachesis said. "But not close enough. Listen to me. *Uhrt Elostrnt Rtincyru.*"

I threw my hands in the air. "That sounds exactly the same!"

"Not quite. The pronunciation of the 'cyr' sound is critical. It is the difference between invoking the gods and demanding a ham sandwich."

"Really?"

She shook her head. "No, not really." There was a long pause. "Our forefathers had no concept of ham, or sandwiches. It would be more like a pocket of meat, filled with meat, but that is not the point."

"It's not?" I scoffed. "I never thought I'd want to know how to order a ham sandwich if I'm ever sent back in time, but here we are."

Lachesis grimaced. "Do it again. Enunciate every syllable."

I sighed. "*Uhrt Elostrnt Rtincyru.*"

She gave me a stern look. "Again."

"*Uhrt Elostrnt Rtincyru.*"

Her timber rose in excitement. "Once more."

"*Uhrt Elostrnt Rtincyru.*"

"That's it!" Lachesis said with glee in her voice. "That's it. Now, for the hand sign. I'll get Clotho."

"Wait!" I clutched my stomach as a great pain shot through it. "Can we please take a break? We've been trying this for hours."

Lachesis moved to the stairs. "And we'll be doing it for hours more. You only have one chance when you reach the center of Urgu, and I won't have you mucking it up."

"Fine," I grunted. "We'll keep going, but you have to answer me a question, first."

Lachesis chuckled. "I don't have to do anything."

"That's not true," I replied. "You *have* to keep spinning your quilt."

She shook her head. "That's where you're wrong. I don't have to do it. I am compelled to do it."

"Then compel yourself to do this, too."

"Fine. What do I have to do? Hop on one leg? Eat a banana?"

I shook my head. "Nothing like that. Just answer a question for me."

Lachesis stroked her chin. "That's a mite bit harder, depending on the question, but ask it."

My head rose to meet hers. "I need to know what happened with Hera?"

She shook her head. "That is bad blood. I don't wish to relive it."

"Too bad. You want my help. I want to know."

After a long silence, Lachesis relented, and locked eyes with me. "It was a hundred years ago, almost to the day, when Hera came to us. Hypnos was gone, and we worried about what to do, and we worried about our safety. We always had him for guidance but right then we felt as though we were on our own, alone as we had ever been."

I nodded slowly. "And then Hera came."

"And then Hera came. She promised us everything. She

promised us safety, and she promised us freedom."

"Freedom?"

"Freedom from this place. All we had to do was help her reach the Heart of Urgu, and she would free us from our position, and allow us to roam around the Dream Realm unencumbered by our burden. In ten millennia in service to the gods, none had treated us as well."

"So, you helped her."

"Sadly, yes," Lachesis said in a whisper. "Until we realized what she really wanted. She wanted to use the power of the Heart to shred the Dream Realm apart and use that power to open a door to Earth. We couldn't allow it, so we used the power of the Heart to banish her from the middle of the planet, and cast out the Dreamers, forever."

"Hera must have been pissed."

"That's an understatement. But we managed to get her out of the Spindle and lock our doors so she could never come back, and so that we would never be tempted by her again. And then, we waited, knowing that one day there would be someone to turn back on the lights, and let the Dreamers back in. I just hoped you would come before it was too late."

She placed her hand on mine, and I smiled at her. "I'm not too late. Thank you for sharing your story with me."

"You are our sister." Lachesis smiled. "Bound here with us, and as such, I suppose you should know what Hera is capable of."

I stood up. "All right, you filled your end of the bargain. Now go get Clotho to teach me the hand sign."

She nodded. "Very well. I hope you are dexterous, because you will need to be if you want to complete the formation she will teach you."

"Bring it on."

CHAPTER 15

RED

Boudica and I paddled across the sand ocean in our little dinghy. There was no way to tell for exactly how long we rowed. Time made no sense in the Sandlands because Sekhmet did not allow any darkness in her realm. She insisted upon it, in honor of her sun god, Ra,

"Hurry! Hurry! Hurry!" I shouted as we paddled harder and faster. The boat had started to take in sand some time ago, and Boudica tried to bail us out while I kept paddling, but it was no use. The sand overtook Boudica's ability to bail it out, and we began to sink. The only thing that mattered was making it to shore before we sank into the abyss.

There was a small town on the horizon, and we paddled toward it until it was on top of us. We smashed into the shore just as the stern of the ship fell into the sand. I leapt from the boat onto solid land and grabbed Boudica's arm to pull her up after me. When we were both safely on shore, I looked back across the sea. I could no longer see the Land of Oz, or the Gates of Itherium.

"That sucked," I said, and Boudica nodded along with me.

"We should be dead," she added.

I grinned. "I could say that just about any day of my life."

Boudica slapped me on the back. "And that is why we are friends. Now come, we must find a guide in town to lead us to the Cave."

"I thought you were an expert tracker."

"I am, but it's better to have a guide, if we can find one, especially if there is war afoot."

She pulled an amber crystal out of her pocket and held it up to the sky, where it glowed against the horizon.

"What is that?" I asked.

"Legend says that this crystal will lead us to the diamond in the rough, who will guide us to the Cave of Wonder, the living tomb of Hypnos."

I scoffed. "Sounds like magic bunk to me."

"Isn't all of it, even the true magic, at least partially bunk?" Boudica asked.

"Touché."

Boudica held up the crystal toward the sun. A beam formed on the ground, then tilted up toward the makeshift town. There were little more than two dozen tents surrounding a large black Obelisk in the middle of town. The beam of light illuminated a large tent. Two old men stumbled out of it drunk, falling over each other, and tripping over their own feet.

"Our guide is in that tent," she said. "Or will be soon enough."

"Assuming the legend is right," I replied. "And they rarely are."

"Assuming any of this is right. We're following a

whisper of a hunch, passed down through a hundred travelers before it reached my ears, and my memory in recounting it properly. Now come."

Boudica led me across the encampment. Against the white cloth of the Sand people, her black clothing made her stand out more than usual. Her unkempt, neon-laden hair contrasted sharply with the covered faces of all we passed. Their eyes were the only thing visible for us to know they were following our movements.

Boudica pushed open the flap to the tent. Inside, a dozen men and women cavorted, drunk off their faces, laughing loudly, sitting on pillows and rugs. In the back of the tent, a camel stood behind a makeshift bar made of driftwood from the boats that didn't make it across the sea. A monkey wearing a fez poured drinks.

When we entered, a fat woman playing an oboe in the corner stopped and looked at us, as did everybody else in the place. Finally, an old man blew a puff of smoke into the air, distracting the guests, and everyone went back to doing what they were in the first place, drinking and cavorting.

"This is my kind of place for once," Boudica said, slapping me on the back. "Not stuffy like the Land of Oz."

Boudica walked up to the bar and sat down cross legged on a purple pillow. I stood next to her until she pulled me down to her level. I found a blue pillow beside her and sat down.

"What can I get you?" the monkey asked.

"We are looking for someone," I said.

"Yes, we all could tell from the fact you don't belong here. Who is it? A criminal? A bail jumper? A sand salesman?" He laughed at the last line, as did the camel and two people at the bar next to us. "We have all kinds of criminals here."

"Nothing like that," I replied. "We're looking for...gods, this sounds stupid. A diamond in the rough? Any idea what that means?" The monkey looked at us with a quizzical expression, furrowing his brow. I turned to the bar patrons, who all seemed to be eavesdropping on our conversations. "Anybody? Diamond in the rough?"

The collective reaction of the assembled drunks ranged from confusion to indifference, but not a hint of recognition on any of their faces.

Boudica held out her stone. "This is what led us here."

The monkey looked at it and laughed. "That's just amber. It will lead you all over the desert, wandering for years like Moses, until the sand swallows you up. I'm afraid you've been had, my dear. You're the fifth person to come this month looking for some sort of answer to their quest, and all of them left disappointed."

Boudica slammed her fist on the bar. It creaked and wobbled as the other patrons tried to keep it upright. "I don't like to be disappointed."

The monkey went back to pouring drinks. "I don't know what to tell you. There's nobody like that here, at least not anyone that I know, and I know everyone."

"We can wait," I said.

"You'll be waiting a long time," the monkey replied.

"We already have," Boudica added with a bitter note. "Meanwhile, bring us two of the strongest drinks you have, and don't dawdle."

CHAPTER 16

ROSE

Jamil pulled up to a dilapidated strip mall outside of Sacramento and turned off the car. I thought she was joking when she finally stopped, but then I remembered that nothing she had ever done was funny, and I realized she expected us to take the next step in our Dream Realm journey in a place where the least gross store said "Et S op" on the window.

"Come on," Jamil said, getting out of the car. "This is what you wanted."

"No." I trudged along behind her. "I wanted help putting my soul back together, not getting tetanus."

Jamil rolled her eyes. "Look, I've only ever met one super powerful demon, and he runs this pet shop."

I furrowed my brow. "How powerful a demon could he be if he runs a pet store in Sacramento?"

"That's a fair point," Jamil replied. "But he's still the most powerful demon I know. He's also kind of stuck in the body of a human, so try not to bring that up when you see him, no matter how freaky he looks."

"I hate this already," I replied, following Jamil into the store.

The inside of the store was worse than the outside. The earth had begun to retake the store. Dirt poured in along the edges, large vines wrapped around the display cases and the empty cages, once full of puppy mill pets now lay empty. Something told me this wasn't the kind of place that cared about the plight of breeder dogs, so I was quite sure they used mills.

"Despite our appearance, we are open."

The stilted voice was coming from the back of the store, where a dusty counter held up a register and an assortment of knick-knacks. A tall man stood up behind the counter and studied us. Every move he made looked unnatural, like it hurt, as if he were the guy in *Men in Black* wearing an "Edgar suit." His face drooped down and looked pasty gray, as if he hadn't seen the sun in three hundred years, and he glistened from sweat.

Jamil walked up to the counter, nonchalant, as if we didn't just see the oddest human in the entire world. "Etsop, do you remember me?"

Etsop nodded. "I remember all who patronize my shop, wood nymph, and now I believe you are patronizing me by returning here with another."

Jamil beckoned me forward. "This isn't just anybody. This is the Dreamer that the Gorgon went into the Nightmare Realm to find. Do you remember the Gorgon? The one from the last time I was in here?"

Etsop's neck jittered as he cocked his head to the side and studied me. "Fascinating. So, it worked, or at least in a way. Lovely to meet you." His hand rose like it was being lifted by a string. "And you are charmed, I'm sure."

I held out my hand, and Etsop clasped it lightly. "I am charmed."

"Hrm," Etsop said, wrinkling his brow. "It's interesting that the Gorgon would go in to find one so...ordinary."

I pulled my hand back. "That's not very nice."

Etsop looked at me with a curious expression, as if he were trying to understand how I could be offended by his statement. "I'm sorry, my dear, but in my line of work you meet every type of creature, and humans are the most ordinary of them all. That she would risk so much for you must mean humanity has something that I overlooked...or she did."

"I'm afraid we came for more than a meet and greet," Jamil said.

"Of course. Nobody comes for a visit anymore." The demon seemed genuinely saddened by the observation. "What can I do for you?"

I stepped forward. "I need to put my soul back together, and I need you to help me return to the Dream Realm."

"Ah, your soul. So that is why you look so out of sorts. Well, of course I could help you, I could, but I'm afraid there is a problem."

"What problem?"

Etsop slapped his gums together. "You see, your paramour owed me a favor, and I simply can't help you until you fulfill her obligation to me, especially with the precarious nature of entering the Dream Realm, and mending souls."

"I'm not going to kill anyone," I said.

"Of course not," Etsop replied. "Perish the thought. Humans are so frail you do a fine job killing yourselves." Etsop reached under the table and gingerly pulled out a black box. "I simply need you to deliver this package."

"That's it?" I replied. "Can't you just hire FedEx or something?"

Etsop's finger traced along the edge of the box. "I'm afraid not. This is delicate and I can only trust it to one who owes a debt to me."

"Seems simple enough." I reached for the package, but Jamil smacked my hand away.

"Wait!" Jamil exclaimed. "What's in it?"

Etsop wagged his finger gently. "I can't tell you that, but I promise you it will do no harm to either of you, or anyone else. It won't get you arrested, or damn your eternal souls, broken as they may be."

"What if I say no?" I asked.

"Then I cannot help you. And I promise, you need my help."

I scoffed. "There are other demons."

"Yes, but there is a problem—a complication, if you will. Your soul is broken. It is like a magnet for those creatures who...let's just say that keep the world in order. You are an anomaly, and should you not get help soon, they will find you." He sighed, looking at his strange hands. "I don't envy what they will do to you if they do."

"Why?" I asked. "What happens if they do?"

"They will clean you."

"That doesn't sound so—"

"Out of existence."

"Oh." I gulped. "Then I guess I will help you."

"Goodie," Etsop reached for a pen and wrote down an address on a piece of paper. "Just deliver this package to this address. Room 1036. Ask for Herbert Milford."

I grabbed the package. It was heavier than I thought it would be, like it was filled with a cinder block, and the package didn't seem to have any creases in it. "And then you'll help me?"

Etsop bowed ever so slightly. "You have my word."

"Then it's a deal."

I turned to walk away, but Etsop called out to me. "Oh yes, and one more thing."

"What's that?" Jamil said. "What else could you possibly want?"

"Just a warning," Etsop said, trying to pull the sides of his mouth into a smile. "If you happen to find a wounded bird on the side of the road, don't let it get away."

CHELLE

I practiced and practiced and practiced the spell the fates taught me until my hands were numb and my arms were bruised. Clotho and Lachesis were relentless. In the moments I wasn't tending to my responsibilities weaving the Quilt of Life, I studied the perfect technique for the spell. Eventually I figured it out and was able to perform the move to their exacting specifications.

It was more unforgiving than any spell I had ever been taught. Usually, you could mess up slightly, get the gist right, and still make a half-hearted cast of a spell, but this was different. It was brutally exacting if you got it wrong, and even more so if you got it right.

Every time I performed the spell, my body ached and my hand swelled. I felt a fire burning in my stomach, and a whimper escaped my mouth. I shook and felt as if my body was breaking apart with every word. That's how I knew I was doing it right. When I didn't, I merely felt a slight tingle, but when I did it right, my soul felt like it was separating from its body.

Will this spell kill me?

That was the question I was desperate to ask, and finally one night I was able to ask while we were sewing patches into the Quilt of Life. I had gotten quite good at sewing, just as the fates claimed I would. The exercises that Clotho put me through to learn the spell technique made my fingers nimble and my body lithe. I could sew two patches together in seconds, and soon I was able to catch up on all the patches that had piled up during my studies. It wasn't impressive, as I had the easiest job of the three, but I was still proud of my improvement.

"Who will take over for me while I am in the middle of Urgu?" I asked. It wasn't the question I really cared about, but I had to warm up to it.

"We will take turns doing your job," Clotho replied.

"And there will be another, eventually," Lachesis added. "There is never an empty seat for long."

"No, never," Clotho said.

"But I will come back, won't I?" I asked. Both Clotho and Lachesis stared down at their work. Neither could look me in the eyes. "Won't I?"

Lachesis sighed. "Sew. Your stitches are sloppy."

I threw down the quilt. "I don't care about this stupid thing. Answer me. Am I going to die down there?"

There it was. I couldn't shake the feeling that there was always more that they weren't telling me. Lachesis was always deferential with me. Clotho was more open, and she still couldn't look at me.

"Sew," Clotho said. "You don't want to get behind."

"Who cares?" I shouted, standing up. "Does any of this matter? I mean, what will happen if you aren't there to cut the string, Clotho? And you, Lachesis, to weave it?"

Lachesis sighed. "Then they will be forgotten."

"So?" I said.

"Sew," both of them answered.

"No," I replied. "Not until you tell me what's going to happen to me."

Lachesis and Clotho both looked at each other. Finally, Lachesis met my gaze. "We don't know."

"The path forward is foggy for us, especially when it deals with our direct involvement." Clothos said, biting her lip. "We can only see what is in front of our noses, which is how we know you must go, and you alone."

"But we do not know what will happen then," Lachesis stated. "But that spell—"

"It's meant to kill me."

"Not necessarily," Lachesis replied.

"It's pure power," Clotho said. "I've never known any, none except a god, that can contain that power without breaking apart. Even to say the words—"

I grabbed my chest with my hand. "It feels like I'm being ripped in half."

"Yes," Lachesis said. "That is true power that cannot be contained, and it is surging through you."

"Now sew," Clotho said.

I sighed. "What are we even doing here?" I sat back down. "Why do I have to do this?"

Clotho blinked slowly. "Because none of us could go."

I knew the next line. "Because you don't have bodies."

"Yes, and that is the extra battery you have, and why you will succeed where we would surely fail."

I looked down at the patches in my hand. "Does any of this even matter?"

Clotho sighed. "We do not know, but it is our task, as restarting the world is yours. Now sew."

There was no more arguing with them. All that was left

was the wait to fulfill my destiny, or what felt like my destiny. The world had always tried to kill me, and yet I kept living, for what, for why? To die at the right time, for the right reason? *Was that enough for a life?*

CHAPTER 18
AINE

You can't escape me.

Agrona's voice echoed through my brain as I reappeared in my fairy castle buried deep in the Enchanted Woods. Hera's shadow demons attacked mercilessly and, though my soldiers fought bravely, they were no match.

"Captain!" I screamed, seeing the battalion of soldiers defending the throne room. My majestic pink walls that had stood for a thousand years had been scraped clean and replaced with either black dust or the cracked façade underneath.

A black fairy clad in silver sparkles turned to me. "My queen! You've returned!"

"You must retreat, Elfred!"

Elfred shook his head. "The castle has not been undefended in a thousand years and I won't have it fall on my watch!"

"You are foolish! Brave, but foolish." I pointed in the direction of the Emerald City. "Your queen orders you to fall back to the Emerald City. Get as many citizens into the keep as you can and defend it. The magic there should protect you."

"And what of you?" he asked.

Yes. What of you?

I squeezed the golden book. "Get them to the castle, Captain. Don't fail me."

He nodded. "Yes, ma'am."

I disappeared again, this time to the throne room of the Emerald City. The Mountain People huddled on the floor as the shadow demons flew and crashed into the walls. Hera had called off her demons during her last attack, but her death must have set them free to rampage again.

"Balor!" I screamed, and the bushy red-headed man rushed forward.

"Yes, my queen?" Balor replied.

"Am I your queen?"

"Of course."

I fluttered up to his face. "Then, defend this castle for me. Allow my fairies to enter the throne room. They will help you gather people from the Emerald City within its gates. Do not let it fall while I am gone."

"Where will you go?" Balor asked.

I clenched the golden book in my hands. "There must be someone, somewhere, who can read this, and I aim to find them."

Smart. Agrona's voice echoed. *But I will drive you mad before you reach salvation.*

"No," I replied. "I will go to the one place that is madder than you could ever drive me."

There was only one place that could drown out Agrona's incessant prattling. A place shrouded in fog and confusion. A place where no sane person would dare tread.

You wouldn't...

But I was already gone from the castle, reappearing in the plains of the Spider; inside Anansi's Mists of Madness. His entire kingdom rested there, where you would lose yourself in time and space. The fog made you lose your way. It didn't let you see more than two inches in front of you, but that was nothing compared to the tricks it played on your mind. None who survived the Bogs was sane enough to talk about what they saw, and here I was, willingly entering the madness, with Anansi's help being my last hope.

The spider god had little use for human or monster kind, and he despised the forked tongue of fairies, especially the Unseelie. I had to hold out hope that he hated one thing more than all of us—Agrona, and that he knew more about the golden book.

Otherwise, I was doomed to wander the mists forever. They already had an effect on my psyche, for I had forgotten how to return to the castle. Soon I would forget everything else about my life, or have it used to drive me mad as a hatter.

Hopefully, I could find help before that happened, though help was not easy to find in the mists.

CHAPTER 19
NIMUE

"How long have you been here, Gorgon?" I asked as we sped through the Nightmare Realm. She pushed along with her tail while the group of newly-freed Dreamers and I held tightly to her back.

The Gorgon laughed, cradling the glowing green spider egg under her arm. "My name is Esther, and I've been here since I was murdered and harvested for organs."

"That's horrible," I said, disgusted. "Why would anyone do that to you?"

She turned toward me. "Was monster hunting not big business when you were alive?"

I sighed. "I wouldn't know. When I was on Earth my life was quite ordinary. I miss it."

"Being ordinary?"

"Earth," I replied. "But yes, perhaps I miss that, too. I used to think power was a great gift, but I am beginning to believe it is a curse. Maybe I will be a simple bar wench when I return to Earth again."

"If you return."

"I will return, Esther," I said. "You can count on that. It has consumed me for eons, and I always get what I desire."

"Not yet, you haven't." Esther smiled.

Esther leaned back and carried us upwards on the slope of a cliff. It was illuminated by neon flowers growing along its face. The Dreamers gasped, clinging tightly to each other as we moved into the dark sky speckled with neon stars.

"Where are we going?" I asked.

"Home," Esther replied.

We rose to a cliffside that overlooked the vast nothingness of the Nightmare Realm. Once my eyes adjusted, I could see that it wasn't nothingness at all. There were vast canyons and undulating valleys, and even towns twinkling on the horizon.

"Everyone off," Esther said, when she'd come to a stop. "It's beautiful, isn't it?"

I stepped to the ground and looked out over the valley. It was truly quite beautiful in its way, though its way was a horrific way. "It's something, all right."

"Once you get used to it, it's not much different than Urgu, or Earth. There are beings trying to live in any way they can. Some are feral, others less so. But you can have the same view from every place on every plane of existence. There's something comforting about that."

I sighed. "And yet, we still had to save a bunch of souls from a spider."

"Yes," Esther nodded. "It is quite a bit more dangerous here than other places, I'll give it that. But every now and then, in the stillness, there is beauty to it. Now come. I have something to show you."

Esther slithered into a cave behind us. I followed her through the serpentine corridors lit only by the neon flowers. I heard some type of chattering, and it grew louder as we moved further down into the abyss.

My ears perked up, and a shiver crawled down my spine. "What is that?"

I readied for a fight, but Esther raised her hand to stay my fears. "Just wait. We are safe here."

She was a monster, and yet I trusted her. No monster would risk their lives to save people from a spider's nest just to eat them alive, right? Or maybe a very stupid monster would. A hungry, feral, deceitful one, perhaps, and Gorgons certainly fit that description.

Esther stopped. Her hands rose high into the air. "Move."

The cave rumbled, and something big shifted in the distance, revealing a light at the end of the tunnel and turning the volume up on the chatter. Esther turned to us, and we gathered around her.

"You are stuck here in the Nightmare Realm, and I am sorry about that. There is no way back home, except to parlay with a demon. Even if you could find one, they would demand your soul in exchange for dastardly deeds. More likely, you will die before you find one. Luckily, there are others like you, and given time, you can create a life for yourself here like I have, and like so many before you. It will take some adjustment, but I come to offer you a home here."

She turned and slithered down the cave without another word. We followed behind her until we reached the end of the corridor, where it emptied into a great cavern filled with people and music. It was divided into five levels, with houses and shops on each one. The bioluminescence of the plants lit the cave, and in the center a large bonfire roared. People ate and cavorted around the flames.

Hundreds of people walked the different levels of the cavern, talking, laughing, and carrying on with their day as if they weren't stuck in a walking nightmare. When the last of those we saved were inside the cavern, Esther turned back to the entrance and raised up her hand.

"Close."

A boulder rolled in front of the opening to cover it up. Then, Esther turned to a group of humans who walked up to her.

"My friends," Esther said with a smile. "So good to see you."

"And you." The woman was wearing thick glasses and a thick fur coat. She brightened when she saw the group of us standing there. "I see you brought new guests for us."

"I did, Annie," Esther said to her. "Will you show them around?"

Annie replied with a polite, warm smile. She turned to the two people behind her. "William and John, please take our new residents around and show them the ropes."

The two men walked toward the small group of us with their hands extended in greeting, but Esther moved in front of me. "Not this one. I'll show her around personally."

"Of course," one of the men said before they both walked past toward the others in the group.

"Come," Esther said to me, continuing on the path. "There is much to do."

Everybody in the makeshift town knew Esther and smiled graciously at her with a reverence usually reserved for popes and gods.

"You are quite well liked here," I said as we walked.

She chuckled. "It only took me dying, being the least hideous thing accursed to walk this land, and then saving their lives before people realized I might not be so bad after all." She sighed deeply and loudly, as if to unburden herself from pain she refused to speak.

"How did you find this place?" I asked.

"It was my first home here. Then, one day, some hapless man walked in, scared out of his gourd, and I offered him sanctuary. More and more people came, and then I started to find them all around the Nightmare Realm. There are millions out there I can't help, but I try to focus on those that I can."

"These people seem to like you very much," I said. "I don't think I've ever been looked at the way these people look at you."

She nodded graciously. "It is an honor to finally be seen for my true self. Now, we have to get you some new clothes."

"New clothes?" I asked, confused. "Are we going to a fashion show?"

Esther shook her head. "If you are to be seen out in the Nightmare Realm, you can't look like you just stepped out of a ball." She pointed to the gown I wore to Rose's coronation, a large black gown I had yet to change out of. I was ill prepared for a journey. "You'll need to look like the nightmares you hope to encounter, or they will eat you alive. I have watched too many good men and women die to let it happen to you."

I cocked my head. "How do you know I am good?"

She didn't return my gaze, instead looked out toward the cavern. "I smelled it on you."

"Smelled it?"

"You have the scent of my daughter on you. You know my Chelle."

Chelle. The Gorgon I'd tried to kill and maim several times. My nemesis, and this was her mother. Of course she was. I would deal with that in my due time, but for now I had to play coy and make nice or I would be lost in the Nightmare Realm without a friend, as temporary as our relationship might be. She had use to me, yet.

"You do know her, do you not?" Esther asked.

I nodded after a long pause, deciding the only truth was to embrace the lie. "She was one of my dearest friends and closest allies."

Esther smiled. "Then, you are family to me."

I returned the smile. "I haven't had a family in many centuries."

As I said those words, I realized they were true, and it made me sad in a profound way. I put a brave smile on my face and blinked away the tears that tried to form in my eyes.

Esther slapped her hands together. "Now, you are part of ours, and I will do all in my power to make sure you find Epiales. It is the least I can do for one who helped my daughter."

Helped her. Tried to kill her. All the same thing in the end. "Thank you."

CHAPTER 20

RED

Boudica and I sat in the bar tent, waiting for a diamond in the rough. We drank for hours, laughing and cavorting like old times, when Ozma still sat on the throne, and Hypnos hadn't abandoned us.

"I will admit, I have missed this," Boudica said. "You are a good companion."

"I have missed it as well."

We both stared off for a long moment, each lost in our own thoughts. That's when I noticed a little thief grab Boudica's amber stone that she had set on the table. In one motion I grabbed the dagger from my belt and stabbed the knave's sleeve with it, pinning him to the bar.

"Thief!" I shouted.

Boudica jumped up, her stool clattering behind her, and I studied the fresh-faced boy in front of me. He couldn't have been more than sixteen—at least when he came to Urgu. Time mattered little in the Dream Realm. He could have been a thousand or a hundred, and his looks would never have changed.

"I just wanted to look at it," the boy said. "I wasn't gonna steal it."

"Bullshit!" the monkey bartender said. "He's a pickpocket and a nuisance. Now, can you get your knife out of my bar?"

I pulled the knife out and sheathed it in my belt again. "Sorry about that," I said to the bartender.

Boudica grabbed the boy by the collar of his jacket and held him in the air. The rest of the bar turned to look, amused at the scrape the boy had gotten himself into, without a shred of anger or concern on their faces.

"What of the gem?" Boudica asked. "Tell me all you know."

"I recognize it," the boy said. "I have the same one. They could be twins."

The whole bar laughed. A man with a scruffy beard and salted hair called out. "You ain't owned anything in your whole life, Aladdin, you nasty sand rat!"

"Looks like nobody here believes you," I said. "And that doesn't fare well for us believing you, either."

"I swear," Aladdin said, kicking his feet helplessly in the air. "I found one just like it in the desert. It led me across the dunes to a cave at the border of the Mountain. I could not open it no matter how hard I tried."

"A cave?" Boudica asked. "What of this cave?"

Aladdin scrunched up his face, trying to concentrate while he struggled against Boudica's hands. "It had strange markings that I couldn't understand. I stayed there for days trying to open it, until monsters from the Mountain Realm scared me off."

Boudica looked at me and nodded. We were both thinking the same thing. We had found our guide, no matter how little I could believe it. She dropped Aladdin to the ground. "Show me this rock."

Aladdin scrambled back to standing and reached into his pocket. He withdrew a red crystal that looked remarkably similar to Boudica's. "See. I told you."

"What's your name, boy?" Boudica asked, looking from the crystal to the boy's face.

He smiled at us, even though he was in grave peril. "Aladdin, ma'am."

I smiled back, appreciative of his spirit if not his methods. "Congratulations, Aladdin. You've just volunteered to be our guide. Take us to this cave."

Aladdin shook his head vigorously. "Are you crazy? There's a war going on in the North. I ain't going back there. I'll die!"

I pulled my daggers and dug them into Aladdin's hip hard enough to make my point, but not hard enough to break skin. "We could kill you now."

"You wouldn't," Aladdin grunted. "You'd be arrested."

I looked around. The people in the bar turned back to their drinks. One of them laughed and shook his head. "I don't think anybody would care if you were dusted."

Aladdin gulped. "Fine, but if I die, it's your fault."

Boudica took a sip of beer. "We can live with that."

CHAPTER 21
AINE

I was lost in the Mistreach.

Of course I was lost. The Mistreach was nothing but fog and grass, as far as the eye could see, which was barely past the nose on my face, incidentally. At least the pounding in my head from Agrona's incessant nagging had subsided now that she couldn't find me. Of course, I couldn't find me either, which meant that I couldn't find Anansi, or the king of the Mistreach. I held my breath, trying to avoid breathing the mists of insanity that worked to fill my lungs. If I took one breath, I would surely lose myself in this strange place.

The Mistreach was the most secretive of all the areas of Urgu. Once Anansi took control of it, he covered it in a thick haze that would drive any who entered into an insane, chattering mess. The thing the Mistreach wanted most was to be left alone. The people who lived there didn't interact with any others. Luckily, it didn't matter much. They didn't cause trouble, and they didn't want trouble. The Mistreach needed no trading partners. Of course, that made them the poorest area of Urgu.

"Are you lost?" a shaky, male voice called out.

A dim orange light cut through the fog as it neared me, and suddenly, I could see several feet in front of me, all the way to an old, black man standing in a field of brown grass. His knees knocked and his arms were so frail I barely believed that he could hold up his lantern. His white beard hung down to his belly button, and his green eyes pierced through the fog. "It's okay. You can speak when the mist clears."

I took a small breath, and when I didn't go insane, I took a deeper one. "Depends. Are you friendly or a hallucination?"

"That depends," the voice replied, raspy and deep. "Are you?"

"I am friendly if you are."

"And I am if you are," the shaky voice replied. "Are you lost?"

"You might say that," I replied, shifting the golden book in my arms. "Though, admittedly I'm lost by my own volition."

The man pointed into the mist. "Well, my inn is a little bit up the road. You're welcome to come and sit until you find your bearings."

"Is this how you sell rooms to your inn?" I asked. "Finding lost souls in the mist?"

"That's one way," he replied. "Another way is that I don't need much, so when I don't get much, I don't mind much."

The old man shuffled through the grass, and I fluttered to catch up with him. "How does your light work to dispel the fog?"

The old man shrugged. "Don't think you'd care much to

hear about it. The end result is all that matters, isn't that right?"

I shook my head. "Well, if it's not a good story, then I suppose not."

"Do you want to hear a good story? Have you heard the one about how brother Anansi ended up in Urgu?"

I shook my head. "No. Must have been before my time."

The man took in a deep breath, settling in to tell the tale. "Anansi was a powerful god. Perhaps too powerful, some say."

"Do you say that?" I asked.

"Please don't interrupt. This is my story, so everything I say is something I say. Do I interrupt you when you are telling stories?"

"Well, frankly, I don't know," I replied. "We've only known each other a couple of minutes."

The man sighed. "Do you want me to continue?"

"Please."

"Then shut up. Anansi was a powerful god. The most powerful god in all the world, some said. His father Nyame, the great sky god, was there at the beginning, helping Zeus and Odin create the universe. Anansi, for his part, preferred the company of humans. Do you know why that is?"

After a long moment of him staring at me, I spoke again. "Am I supposed to answer? I don't want to be rude."

The man nodded. "Yes, when I ask a question, you can answer. Do you know why brother Anansi preferred the company of humans?"

"No, I don't."

"Because they were so easy to trick, like babies." The man giggled at himself. "And Anansi, powerful as he was, and just as he was, loved trickery. He never met a prank he didn't enjoy, the more intricate the better."

"Sounds mean."

"Oh, come now. His tricks were never devious, and a little prank never hurt anyone. Unfortunately, the other gods were not so good natured. They were cruel to humans, using them in devious and deceitful ways."

"That tracks," I cut in when the old man paused to take a breath. "From my experience with them at least."

He gave me a sideways glance, and then opened his mouth to continue. "Anansi did not like this, so he decided to get even with the gods, and give them a taste of their own medicine. He planned a trick, a great deception that would quake the heavens. But something went wrong, and in the execution of his plan, Nyame died. It was an accident, but the gods found him too irrational to stay with them, and too powerful to banish, so, they sent him here to this place."

"That's a pretty okay story," I said to him. "Why the mist, though?"

A small cottage appeared in the distance, at the edge of the light. The old man turned back to me. "That is a story for another time."

"What is your name, stranger?"

The old man nodded. "Isiah, my dear." He hissed when he said it, like the name burned his tongue. "You can call me Isiah."

I nodded politely. "Thank you, Isiah. I'm grateful for shelter."

"Don't thank me yet. You haven't seen the inside. I do appreciate your kindness, though. Now come, I'll make some stew to warm your bones."

ROSE

Demons were stupid. That's one thing I had learned from my short time with Etsop. He could have forced me to do anything in the world, and all he wanted me to do was deliver a package to Reno? *What a waste of my time.*

"And what was that thing he said about a little bird?" Jamil said from the passenger's seat as we drove. Neither of us shut up about our strange meeting with the demon since we left, and even though we were playing the same conversation on repeat, it helped pass the time.

"Maybe we should turn on some music, or a podcast." I said, reaching for the radio.

Jamil sighed. "No podcast. Just music. I know all you've got is politics, and I'm not interested in hearing about whether we're going to get into WWIII. I know it's going to happen any day now, and I just...want to live in ignorance. Is that so bad?"

I cocked my head. "Kind of. I mean we all live in this world, man. It's our duty to figure out how to do it well and not screw it up."

Jamil leaned back into the headrest with a sigh. "You sound like my brother."

"You have...a brother?" I hadn't thought of monsters having siblings or families before. Jamil was a wood nymph, but the medallion she wore around her neck cast an illusion that made her look like a human. I hated that monsters like Jamil and Chelle had to cover up their identities, but it was necessary in a world full of psychotic apes. They couldn't afford to look different. It was bad enough being the wrong skin color, or looking the wrong way, or having the wrong accent, but to be the wrong species was basically a death sentence.

"Yeah, I have a few. Trees reproduce. He's...gone most of the time, like the rest of my family."

"What does he do?"

But Jamil didn't answer, instead, she sat up, rigid in her seat, and watched the car speeding up on my left side to pass us. She flung her hand toward the window, pointing. "Holy—what is that?"

I whipped my neck around to look, but it just looked like a plain car to me. A black sedan with glass windows and normal tires.

"I don't get it—"

"Look at the driver, man," Jamil whispered.

I squinted. I could see perfectly into the driver's seat, but there wasn't one. The car was being driven by nobody or nothing. "So what?" I shrugged. "That's probably just a Google car or something. They're everywhere."

Jamil shook her head. "I don't think so. Have you ever known them to drive anything without Google logos all over it?"

She had a point. There was nothing on this car, except

the metallic black paint that made it nearly blend in with the darkening horizon.

"No, but so what, Maybe Uber—"

"You ever seen a driverless car without an engineer in the back just in case something goes wrong?"

No, I hadn't. There was always an engineer, just in case. I couldn't panic. Etsop told me that something horrible would be after me if word got out that I didn't have a soul. My mind raced, wondering if this was what he was talking about.

"Rose, look out!"

I snapped out of my daze, but it was too late. I had run off the side of the road, past the rumble strips. The gravel jerked us all over and I had to spin the wheel hard to avoid the electric pole in front of us. I missed the pole, but when I pumped the brakes the car refused to stop turning. We made two full rotations before the car finally lurched to a stop in the ditch that ran parallel to the highway.

Panting, I looked over at Jamil. She was just as scared as I was, out of breath with a frantic look in her eyes.

"You okay?" I said.

"Yeah," Jamil replied, heaving. "What was that?"

I looked back to the road for the car, but it was speeding along as if it hadn't noticed us. I suddenly felt stupid for having a panic attack. I shook my head. "I don't know. Maybe we've been driving too long. Let's get back on the road and figure it out."

The car had stalled in the spin, and when I turned the key, it sputtered and refused to turn over. "Come on!" I shouted, trying it again, but it was no use.

Jamil placed her hand on mine. "It's flooded. We have to call a tow truck."

"Out here?" I squealed. "Who's possibly going to come get us?"

Jamil pulled up her phone and looked through Yelp. "There's one here. Let's see if they're open." The phone rang and I heard somebody pick up. "Yes, we just had an accident out in the middle of 80 between Gold Run and Alta. Can you—Oh you can? Great. Do you take Triple A? No? Well, we'll figure it out."

She hung up the phone. "All right. Now all we have to do is wait."

Brilliant. What could happen to us while we waited? Probably nothing, right? In the middle of the desert, nobody around for miles. *What could go wrong?*

CHAPTER 23
NIMUE

Esther dressed me in a black body bag with neon stripes down the back, and a large skeletal mask that made me look like a giant bird. Once I was dressed, she dragged me back out of the cave into the Nightmare Realm and traipsed me across the barren wastelands of the haunted continent.

"I feel ridiculous," I said. "I can barely see in this thing."

"It doesn't matter if you can see," Esther replied. "This 'ridiculous' suit will stop you being attacked by the monsters of the Nightmare Realm. I can only protect you so much, and where we're going, I'm not quite the known commodity I am in this region. I've decided to use a hefty amount of caution."

I couldn't argue with her there. I certainly didn't want to be attacked by any more monsters, but I hated being guided at the whim of another person, or monster as the case may be, as had been my lot the entirety of my time in the Nightmare Realm.

First, it was the crazy furry cat with the huge grin, and now the monstrous mother of the girl who hated me most in the entirety of existence. That might be hyperbole, but the fact remained that I wasn't much liked by anyone in the Dream Realm, even my closest supporters.

"Wait here," Esther said. We were in a small clearing surrounded by neon bushes blooming with flowers of every color. They smelled of rotten daffodils and turnips, which was oddly specific and mildly appealing. I sat on the log of a hollowed-out tree as Esther placed her hands behind her back.

I sighed loudly. "What are we waiting for? I don't have time to dilly dally."

"We're not dilly dallying," Esther said. "We're waiting for him to come back."

"Who is him?"

Esther frowned. "Can you just trust me already?"

"Lady," I scoffed. "I don't trust my own mother."

"Fair enough. Sad, but fair." Esther turned to me. "We're waiting for the one who's going to help us find Epiales. His shop is not always in this plane of existence."

"Where is he coming from?"

Esther chuckled to herself, clearly annoyed and perturbed in equal measure. "You ask a lot of questions."

I wrapped my arms around myself. "Only when I'm kept in the dark, literally and figuratively."

Esther sighed. "I don't think you will care even if I explain it to you."

I stared at her intently. "Try."

A flash of white light shot through the clearing and blinded me for a moment. It was the brightest light I had seen since entering the Nightmare Realm. When my eyes could focus again, I saw a quaint shop, tall and wide, standing erect in front of me. Its dark paint and neon veneer blended into the rest of the Nightmare Realm, and I wasn't sure I would be able to find it if I didn't know where to look.

"Ah, here he is," Esther said with a smile. "See, trust. Let's go."

The door to the shop creaked open and a tall, slender man stepped out. No. Man wasn't the right way to describe him. He moved more like a spider, and a jittery one at that, wearing a human skin around him. The man's skin hung loose, and his arms seemed barely strong enough to lift themselves into the air to greet us.

"Welcome, my dear," he said. His words were soft and slow. "So nice to see you again."

"You look well, Etsop," Esther said, before turning toward me. "This is my friend. She needs your help."

The ends of his mouth curled in the most unnatural smile I had ever seen. It was almost as if wires hung from the ceiling and pulled the edges of his mouth up while the rest of it stayed tightly sealed.

He tented his fingers together in front of him. "Well, if Etsop can help you, then he will."

"Come now, Nimue," Esther beckoned me forward. "You do not want to keep the demon king waiting."

"No," I replied. "I suppose I do not."

CHAPTER 24

AINE

Everything I had tried to eat since entering the Dream Realm tasted like sand, but the stew Isiah made while I waited in the lobby of his inn was delicious.

"Do you know the story of Anansi and the carpenter?" he asked.

I shook my head, ravenously eating the third bowl of soup he placed in front of me. "No, I don't." Isiah hadn't stopped telling me stories since I stepped into the Mistreach, but his voice was so soothing that I didn't mind. While he talked, I barely remembered the angry goddess hunting me, or the doomed fate of my subjects.

"Then let me tell you a story," Isiah said. "One day a young carpenter happened upon Anansi's web. He walked face first into it, but instead of yelling and screaming, he turned back to the spider who built it and, not knowing the spider was in fact Anansi, apologized for being so careless. This confused Anansi, who was used to being yelled at when somebody stepped into his web. He spoke to the weary carpenter, which startled the poor man, who had assumed Anansi was just a normal spider. Anansi said,

'How you treat those smaller than you tells me all I need to know about your character.' He offered to grant a wish for the carpenter, but the man just smiled and told him he was okay and left without a word.

"This confused Anansi. Never had a human denied a gift from the gods! Anansi followed him back to his house and watched as the man worked with his hands all day. In the evening, his wife came home, and the man greeted her. The woman was ugly and fat, and that gave Anansi an idea. He walked up to the man and told him that he could make his wife beautiful and desirable. The man smiled and said, 'Then everyone would see her beauty and covet her. Now her beauty is a secret only we share.' The man said no thank you to the god and went inside.

"Some time later, the man's mother came out of the house. She was old and tired, and Anansi could smell death wafting off her. Anansi had an idea and went to the man. He told him that he could make his mother young again. The man just smiled at Anansi and said, 'Mother has led a good life and is ready to sleep.' The man said no thank you and walked away.

"Angry, Anansi went to the man's mother and told her that her son denied her youth. The mother smiled at Anansi and said, 'Good. I am ready to die. I have lived long and seen much. My husband has died, and my children are grown. I have seen all I wish to see.'

"Some time later, the man went out of his house and picked a bushel of flowers. He walked across the village to a grave site and knelt down beside it. There he cried for a lost child, placing the flowers on her grave. Anansi then knew the true desire of the man's heart. He went to him and told him that he could bring his lost child back from the grave. 'You don't understand,' the man said. 'While I wish to see my daughter more than anything, the beauty of life is in the frailty of it.' The man smiled and said no thank you and went on his way."

"I see," I said, trying to hide the boredom on my face that mixed with confusion at why he would tell such a long and pointless story. Still, he was a good host, and if my years as a queen had taught me nothing else, it was how to feign interest in a dull tale.

"Do you see? You do not have to change to be happy. You do not have to yearn to be free." After a long silence, while I finished another bowl of stew, Isiah spoke again. "Do you see the point?"

"No," I said. "That story was horrible. It just…ended."

The man shrugged. "Maybe you will understand in time."

"I get the point. I just don't agree with it. You are a horrible teacher."

Isiah rubbed his head. "I am no teacher. I am but a storyteller."

"And not a good one, clearly," I said. I didn't want to insult him too much, but it was my way. "That wasn't a very good story."

"Ah." Isiah pointed his finger at me. "Perhaps you are not a very good listener."

I smiled. "No. I'm not, unfortunately." I took a long breath. "I need your help, Isiah."

"You've already gotten my help, Aine."

I placed my hand on the golden book I had brought from Agrona's palace. "I need to get this to your king."

"The Mistreach has a guardian, but no king. She sits for Anansi, while the god is indisposed."

I sat up. "Can you take me to her?"

"Why do you want to see her?" Isiah asked.

"Urgu is in a bad way, my friend," I said, looking down at the floor and shaking my head slowly. "There are horrible things coming for the people of the Dream Realm, and I need Anansi to stand with the Land of Oz to defeat the evil that comes for us."

Isiah cocked his head. "And what makes you think that Anansi will hear you? He's set up his realm to remain as isolated as possible from the rest of Urgu."

"That's the problem!" I threw my hands in the air. "Every damned area of Urgu is on its own, cut off from every other area. We can't defeat this evil by ourselves. We have to work together."

Isiah chuckled. "That's rich, coming from Oz. You cut yourselves off from the rest of us with that danged wall eons ago before the rest of us could even set up a life for ourselves."

I held up my hands. "That wasn't me. That was Hypnos. And we both know he can't speak for us. Not until we find him."

"Find him?" Isiah scoffed. "He doesn't want to be found."

I shrugged. "Maybe. But if that's the case, we have to work even harder to keep the peace."

"We have peace right here."

"Not for long." I shook my head. "Right now, Agrona is bringing an army from the Nightmare Realm with Epiales to take over the Dream Realm. Without Hypnos, our only chance is to band together. I need you to bring me to the guardian and have her speak to Anansi for me. Please, help me. I'm not asking for much."

"You may not think that is much, but to my kingdom, it is everything. The guardian does not take intruders lightly."

Isiah wagged a finger at me. "But I like you, so I will do it. In the morning. First, you must sleep."

"I don't need to sleep."

Isiah took a long pause. "It will give you a chance to have a change of heart."

"I won't. I must see your guardian."

Isiah stood. "Let us go, then."

"Thank you."

"Don't thank me yet," Isiah said with a small laugh. "The guardian will most likely kill you."

I smiled. "She can try."

"She will."

CHAPTER 25
CHELLE

Lachesis and Clotho walked me down the winding stairs, through the darkness of the Obsidian Spindle, until they reached the door that led out into Urgu. A rock grew in my stomach.

"Are we finally going outside?" I asked.

Lachesis shook her head. "No."

I already knew that leaving the Spindle was impossible. I was just trying to bring some levity to a situation that desperately needed it. After all, based on the subterfuge of the other two fates, I was walking to my doom, like an idiot. If I lost my sense of humor about it, then what was the point of it all?

Clotho inched behind the stairwell and held her hand up in the darkness, muttering three words. A light extended from her hand, revealing a portico under the staircase. She smiled at me. "Come."

As if I had any other choice in the matter. They were leading me like a lamb to slaughter, and I was letting them. I knew I would probably die, but it was the only way to see Rose again and, barring that, at least let her have a life filled with dreams. I was stuck in the Spindle for the rest of my life, and if I allowed the Dreamers to come into the world, then I would have a chance to see my love again. It was my only option.

"Don't be scared," Lachesis said as we started down another set of stairs, these even steeper and more cramped.

The thing was, even though I was facing certain peril with an uncertain outcome, I wasn't scared. I was anxious, and nervous, but I wasn't scared. I desperately wanted anybody else to be the one who would become the savior of Urgu, but it had to be me for some reason. Because I made the stupid decision to save Rose.

No, it wasn't a stupid decision.

It was the right one. Now, she could live her life a second time. If I had to forfeit mine to make that happen and save the world, then it would be worth it. I had to hope so, anyway.

"What if I chicken out?" I asked.

"Then this land is forfeit," Clotho replied with a deep sigh.

I scrunched my nose. "How do you know, though, since you already said the way forward was hazy?"

"Foresight isn't an exact science," Lachesis said. "Some things we see clearly. Others we don't, and if you don't fix what we broke and restart the center of Urgu, then everything falls into darkness for as long as we can see."

I stopped on the stairs. "What if I don't care?"

Clotho looked up, past me. "Then we can stop now, but I believe your heart is purer than that, purer than any of ours. After all, Atropos would not have sacrificed herself for no reason."

Lachesis nodded. "And you would not have risked yourself if there was not good in your soul."

"Good for Rose, not for some randos."

"You are not just saving random people." Clotho smiled. "You are saving every person, including your Rose."

Lachesis touched my arm. "The Dream Realm is necessary for the safety of all worlds. Otherwise, people will only have nightmares, and then they lose their hope, their sanity. Including your Rose."

"And you're sure this will help her?"

"It will." Clotho nodded. "She dreams, too. Don't you want her dreams to be pleasant, and not full of terror? Don't you want her to live a good, pleasant life?"

"Of course."

"Then think of her when you complete your quest. Yes, you will save humanity, but you will also save Rose. If she is all that matters, then it should be enough."

I sighed. They knew me. "Fine. Let's do it."

Clotho stopped. "We are here." She turned to me. "This is as far as we can take you."

Lachesis grabbed my hand and placed it on the dark wall. "Open."

The light from my hand glowed, and in the dim light a small stone door materialized, surrounded by snakes. Lachesis touched my arm to it, and the eyes of the snakes came to life, glowing red. There was a clicking from behind the door while the snakes uncoiled and locked end to end in a circle. Once they were in place, the door clicked again, and a gust of wind blew out from the other side.

Clotho pulled open the door. "Good luck."

I gulped, ready to meet my destiny.

CHAPTER 26

RED

Aladdin led us through the tent town in the Sandlands, waving at every person he passed. He received no such kindness in return. It wasn't hard to see why. Aladdin was certainly cheery, maybe even charming, but he was a thief. I watched him pocket two dream balls and a scarf from the people we passed, along with a carafe of water from the side of a camel.

Every person in town clinched up when he passed. Honestly, it was rather impressive that he could still steal anything, given that the people were on high alert when he was around, and yet he kept adding to his collections.

"Aren't you worried about being caught?" I asked.

Aladdin shook his head. "I've never cared about anything in my life. Besides, these people know that I return whatever I steal with interest."

"Do you though?" Boudica asked, squinting her neon eyes.

Aladdin nodded. "You two ask a lot of questions." He smirked. "Don't worry about me, though. I've been doing this a long time."

"How long?" I asked.

"Long enough that I don't even remember. I started in the Dark Domain, and then spent some time in the Bogs, before ending up here, roaming the desert, for the past however many years." Aladdin held his hand up and blocked the menacing sun from his eyes. "The days blend into each other in this place."

The sun never set on Sekhmet's empire, just as the sun rarely rose in Agrona's. I spent years in the vast deserts of the Sandlands without knowing where I was or how to get out. The sand dunes all looked the same, and there were few towns. The nomadic people of the Sandlands often packed up and changed direction on a whim. A town you found a week ago could be across the desert by the time you returned, and any tracks were wiped away by the wind.

The Sandlands were like a living organism. In the other areas of Urgu, things were permanent, roughly at least. In Oz, the Bogs, and even the Mistreach—from what we knew about it—cities stayed where cities were built. The Mountain People moved around often, but between the same locations throughout the year for fortification or strategic placement. In the Sandlands, the dunes gave and took at random; people moved for convenience, or boredom, or to escape. Whatever the reason, the people of the Sandlands never stayed put for long.

"Come," Aladdin said. We approached a large tent three times as wide as the others. I heard the cries of monsters inside and when I entered, a dozen enormous pairs of yellow salamander eyes stared back at me.

"Sand salamanders," Boudica said. "They are glorious."

Sand Salamanders were the mode of transport of choice for the people of the Sandlands. They were quick, low to the ground, and could outrun most of the beings that hunted in the endless desert.

"Take your pick," Aladdin said, handing me a scaly saddle that resembled the same hide as the salamanders. They shed their skin every year, and their skin was a prized possession the people of the desert used to make clothing and equipment.

"So, we're stealing them then," I said.

"Not stealing...borrowing. Forever," Aladdin said with a smile, hopping onto a long-footed salamander with green stripes. "Or until I make a surprising return."

Boudica jumped onto a screaming red salamander as it plucked a fly out of the air with its tongue. "Sounds good to me. What is yours is mine."

I reached into my pocket and pulled out three of the most expensive dreams in my possession. They were complete epics that told tales of Dreamers who slayed dragons and rescued princesses, the rarest dreams in all the realm, and the most prized. Usually, dreams stopped after a few minutes, showing only fragments of a memory, but these ones continued for hours.

"Hey!" a gruff voice called out. I turned to see a burly woman waddling up to me on knobby knees. "Are you stealing from me?"

I shook my head as my companions tried their best to disappear. "No, ma'am. We are just admiring your fine steeds."

She put her hands on her hips. "I know a thief when I see one."

"Then you are seeing incorrectly." I held up the dreams in my hand. They sparked pink and shone on the face of the woman, who was instantly captivated by them. "I hoped you might sell them to us, and in return I would pay you handsomely."

"Is that—" she stammered, entranced by the beauty of the dreams. "Are those...dreams?"

"They are." I nodded, knowing her question before she finished it. "And they are priceless, just like your steeds."

"I have never seen one so beautiful before, and you'll give me three, for this ruddy lot?"

"I would, and you would have the knowledge that you helped us immeasurably."

She plucked the dreams from my hand. "Well, then. I think we have a deal. I'll throw in the saddles, too."

"And some weapons!" Boudica added.

"Yes, and some weapons," the woman said. "You must be in some serious trouble."

"Not trouble," I replied. "But we would appreciate it if you didn't tell anyone what transpired here."

She smiled at me, her teeth twisted and brown. "Anything you say, ma'am."

CHELLE

"Lux."

My hands glowed orange fire as I descended the stairs. There was an eerie quiet, save for the sounds of my own feet. No matter how quiet it is, there's usually something to hear: someone breathing, the hum of a computer, a car whizzing by. But here in this cavern there was nothing but the soles of my feet. When I stopped, even that sound died away, leaving me in an oppressive silence.

I hated the silence. It let my mind wander to the darker parts of my soul. I started to think about whether I had the nerve to kill myself for the greater good. Sure, I hated my life sometimes, but I wanted to live. I wanted to breathe the fresh air of Earth again. I wanted to sit next to Rose and eat a pizza. I wanted all of that, and I would never have it again if I gave up my body.

And if I were to chain myself to the fates, I would never have it again. I would be stuck sewing patches of a quilt for the rest of my days, and that was boring enough to make me want to kill myself. At least this sacrifice would let me die with a purpose.

Heck, there was no guarantee that I would even die. Maybe I'd restart the Dreamers' ability to come to Urgu, and the power wouldn't kill me...

All right, Chelle. Now, you're being naïve...and stupid.

But it was possible, still. The fates had told me my future was covered in a layer of haze. Maybe I would be able to live, and then maybe Rose would dream, and in that dream, we would be together again, if only for a moment.

Rose.

If I didn't restart the dreams in Urgu, she would be left with nothing but nightmares. She deserved better.

All we'd ever had was nightmares. I could unlock dreams for the rest of the world, every single person. I didn't care much about that, but I cared about doing it for Rose. It was enough to give me the strength to carry on, to take another step closer to the center of Urgu. When the stairwell ended, I would be face to face with my destiny.

CHAPTER 28
NIMUE

Etsop led us through the back door and into his shop. I had never seen anything like it before. I took off my mask to get a better look at the wonders on the shelves.

Lights hung down from the ceiling, but they were not suspended by magic or lit by candle as they were in Urgu. I leaned close to one, trying to discern what kind of sorcery kept the balls lit.

"What trickery is this?" I asked.

"It's not trickery," Esther said. "It's electricity. We don't need magic to see in the dark on Earth."

"Earth?" I gasped. "Are we on Earth?"

"Not quite," Esther chuckled. "This shop lives in both of our dimensions, which is why Etsop is such a powerful friend. Unfortunately, you need a body to return to Earth, and we are but souls."

"Fascinating. I very much look forward to seeing what else has changed since I last stepped foot on Earth."

"Another time, perhaps," Etsop said. "But first, come."

The cages lining the walls were filled with odd creatures that croaked and groaned and squawked, each one glowing bright green and larger than any bird, frog, or squirrel I had ever seen in all my centuries in Urgu.

"Don't touch anything," Etsop said. "They will kill you."

"I know," Esther said.

"I'm not talking to you," Estop said, staring at me as he sidled behind the counter. "How may I help you?"

"We need to find Epiales," Esther said.

"Don't we all," Etsop said with a mirthless chuckle.

"Yes, but I know you know where he is."

Etsop jerked his hand to his chest. "That is a terrible thing to accuse me of."

"Please," Esther said. "He hated you and you hated him. After all, he's the reason you're in this body, isn't it?"

Etsop growled. "He may have had something to do with it, but that doesn't mean I hate him."

"No," Esther replied. "But you do, right?"

"No comment," Etsop said.

Esther slapped her hands on the counter. "And you've kept tabs on him ever since."

"Possible, but I would never—"

Before he could finish, Esther pulled a satchel off her back and opened it to reveal the egg we had captured from the spider queen. "If you help us, then I will give you this."

"Nefeski's egg. I've coveted these for so long." Etsop gasped, then hunched down to examine it. "Why would you want to find Epiales? His disappearance has led to both of us having much success here. If he were to come back, he would never approve of you helping Dreamers, nor me selling my wares to monsters."

Esther looked over at me. "This woman was a friend to my daughter, and she needs to find him to save her life. I cannot deny her."

Etsop furrowed his brow. "And you will give me this egg if I help you?"

"Yes."

"Do you know what it's worth?"

"I don't care."

"No, you don't." Etsop paused for a moment. "Very well. I suppose I can help you. After all, if I am ever to leave this accursed body then I need to find him, eventually."

Etsop jerked up the divider between us and walked toward his menagerie of monsters. He reached to the top row of cages and pulled down a fat bullfrog, ten times as big as the biggest I had ever seen. It glowed a dark orange when it inhaled, yellow when it exhaled.

"This little guy is very special. He was once the personal companion of Epiales and can track him anywhere." Etsop handed the frog to Esther. "He's ornery and slow, but he will find the Nightmare King."

"I thought the cat was Epiales's companion. He said—" I said, before Etsop threw up his hand.

"Epiales is mercurial and capricious. He changes companions like others change shirts." Etsop scratched lightly under the bullfrog's chin. "Be careful with this one. He is ravenously hungry and will bolt for food in an instant. Keep him fed and you will find Epiales eventually."

"Thank you," I said.

"Don't thank me, honey. You have no idea what you are bringing on yourself." Etsop opened the back door and held it open as Esther scooted out. Before I could follow, he dropped his arm to stop me. "I know what you want."

"I just—"

"And I know who you are, Nimue the Wicked," Etsop said. "Your desires are legendary...and I can help you."

"Help me?"

"Get what you desire." One side of Etsop's mouth rose in an ugly smile. "It will not come cheaply, though."

"What do you need?"

"Just one thing," Etsop said, looking over at Esther. "The ashes of a weeping mother."

His implication was clear. If I wanted to get back to Earth, I needed to kill Esther and bring her ashes back to him. "What if I can't—"

"Then you'll be stuck here forever," Etsop said, dropping his arm so I could pass. "Or dead. Either way, you have no idea what you will unleash on the world by releasing the Nightmare King."

"I don't care."

"I know you don't." The edges of Etsop's lips curled unnaturally. "That's why I like you."

CHAPTER 29
RED

We trekked across the desert for longer than I could keep track. It was impossible to know how many hours had passed because the sun hadn't moved from its position in the top of the sky since we came into the Sandlands. I would only know we'd arrived when a giant battle raged in the distance.

My sand salamander jolted under me and I nearly fell into the sand. Controlling a sand salamander wasn't as easy as controlling a horse. They were wider and heavier, with a much thornier disposition. Mine liked to pull left and had very little motivation to continue moving forward unless I kept throwing food in front of its face.

"Not much further," Aladdin said, but I knew it was a lie. "Just a few more dunes." He had been saying the same thing for the past several hours, or days, whatever it was.

"How do you deal with this oppressive heat?" Boudica asked, holding her dreadlocks off of her neck.

"It's not so bad once you get used to it." Aladdin said.

"Yes, it is," I replied.

"That's true. It is, but you just have to remember this is all an illusion, yes?"

"An illusion?" Boudica said.

"That's right." Aladdin laughed heartily. "Well, we are not truly in the heat, are we? This whole place is simply a dream, and if this place is a dream, then we can do anything, like stop thinking that we are hot."

"That's stupid," I said, trying to jerk my salamander straight. It kept looking off to the left and moaning loudly. "Come on!"

"You are trying too hard, my friend," Aladdin said. "The salamander is ornery and stubborn. It does not like to be guided. It likes to be trusted."

I scoffed. "You expect me to trust a lizard?"

Aladdin laughed. "In this place, it is much smarter than you."

"Well, in most places a lizard is smarter than her," Boudica said with a smile. "Now quit playing around and let's get going."

But I didn't move, and neither did the salamander. Instead, it planted its feet and howled toward the distant sun. "I don't know. I think it's trying to tell me something."

"Yeah, that it's hot." Boudica wiped her brow. "Now let's get—"

Boom! The ground erupted and I was thrown off my salamander. I pushed myself up to stand only to find three huge balls of black fire rising into the air.

"The nightmare realm," Boudica said, breathlessly.

"They've come through the blockade," Aladdin said, rearing his lizard into the air.

"How?" I shouted, pushing up from the ground. "I thought it was being protected by a god."

"Sekhmet can't stop every demon from entering our land."

I pulled the daggers out of my belt and threw back my red hood. The black fire parted and a long snout emerged from inside of it. Orange eyes appeared sunk into the top of the extended nose. Its lips parted, and jagged teeth snapped at the air. As one of them flew toward me, my salamander flipped out his tongue and grabbed it, swallowing it whole.

"Oh my gods," Aladdin said. We waited for the lizard to keel over and die, but all it did was burp, and a bit of black flame flew out, but then it was calm.

"What just happened?" I said.

"Apparently...these salamanders can eat flames," Boudica said.

"Of course," Aladdin said. "They can eat anything."

Boudica turned her salamander toward the black flames and nodded. The salamander flicked out its tongue and took out another monster. The third one chased after me, and I ducked under the belly of my salamander. The lizard's great belly swelled, nearly crushing me, and a croak erupted from it. Its tongue flicked out once more and grabbed the third flame monster. It chewed for a moment, and then the flame disappeared into its belly.

"How—?" I asked Aladdin.

"It's best not to ask with magic," Aladdin said. "Come, let's get going."

I decided that truly was best. Magic was a silly thing. I hopped back on the salamander and grabbed the reins. "I hope that's the craziest thing I see today."

"You have not seen anything yet," Aladdin replied. "We must be nearing the battle lines, which means every nightmare fighting against our forces will be upon us soon."

I surveyed the surrounding land, shielding my eyes

with my hand. Even though we'd had our first taste of the Nightmare Realm since crossing the Sand Sea, I couldn't see the battle anywhere.

"Why can't we make it out yet then, if we are so close?"

"You will soon, I promise you that, and the battle will stretch across the horizon. You will lose the will to continue and want to turn back."

"You don't know us very well, Aladdin," I said with a snicker. "We don't run from anything."

"Yes," Boudica said, leading her salamander over the next dune. I followed behind, ready for this whole adventure to be over, knowing it had barely even begun. "I long for battle."

I didn't, but I wasn't frightened of it, either, especially if entering the fray could help us save Urgu.

CHAPTER 30
AINE

Isiah led me through the fog toward the castle of Anansi, or at least I was pretty sure that was where we were going. I couldn't see very far in front of us. His lantern lit the fog enough for us to make our way through the mist and collapsed around itself once we'd passed.

"Keep up," Isiah said, but his feet were faster than should have been possible. I pumped my wings furiously, but his long strides sped him away from me until the fog kissed my back and curled around my nostrils.

And I inhaled.

As I disappeared deeper into the mist, Isiah vanished from my view, and I found myself back in my castle, glistening and pink, a bastion of culture in the primitive Enchanted Woods.

"Aine, dear," I heard from behind me and turned around to see my mother, eyes sunken from years on the throne. I was not in my own castle, but hers, back before I fell into the Dream Realm eons ago. "Aine, why are you such a disappointment?"

"I—" I didn't have an answer. I didn't understand what

she was talking about. "I'm not, mother. I'm trying to do you proud."

"And yet you abandoned your people," she said, her purple skin glistening. "You will never save them."

I gripped the golden book in my hands. "Don't say that."

"It's true," a voice grumbled. I turned to come face to face with Nimue. "You know you'll never save them. Not that I blame you. Self-preservation is one thing we have in common. I should applaud you."

"No!" Tears streamed from my eyes. "I'm not running away. I'm saving them all. You'll see!"

There was a cackle. "You think they aren't all already dead. That's cute." Agrona's white eyes burned through me and I felt a hand on my shoulder. I turned around and Agrona melted away to the sweet, dark face of Isiah.

"Don't get turned around in here," he said. "You'll never find your way out."

The mist retreated until I breathed clean air. Without the musty smell of the fog invading my nostrils, my eyes cleared, and I smiled a listless smile at him. "Thank you."

Isiah turned around. "Let me tell you a story about my friend Wilson. He went into the mist one day without a lantern and well...he came back thinking he was a kookaburra. You do not want to be caught in that fog for long. You don't know what it does to the mind. Make you think you're a skunk tiger and have you spraying on everything. Not polite."

"I have no desire to be caught in the fog," I said. "Or be here at all. I only wish to meet with Anansi to tell him my side of the story and get him on our side for the upcoming war."

"Then you are in luck," Isiah said. "Because we are here."

The fog lifted and Isiah turned off his lantern, clipping it to his belt loop. A hint of light shone on a massive structure in front of us; a dozen terraces stacked on top of each other, like the temple at Chichen Itza, each terrace smaller than that last, and capped with a square temple on its summit. Intricately carved runes covered every surface. The ziggurat was painted in green and brown to blend in with the misty forest around it, and tree limbs hung over the top levels before they spidered their way back into the fog.

"Though I doubt luck is on your side," Isiah added.

CHAPTER 31
RED

We rode our salamanders across the desert for what felt like an eon. Aladdin kept prodding us along, telling us we were close. The fleeting hope was worse than the punishing heat.

Finally, after untold hours, we came over a ridge and saw a battlefield stretching past the horizon. The sun battled with the dark, and the dark was winning. A golden army stretched from the bottom of the dune to the darkness that engulfed everything beyond it. Thunder boomed into my ears even though we were miles from the front, and lightning crackled through the darkened sky.

"There it is," Aladdin said. "Come, we'll have to talk to the captain if you wish to enter the battle."

I frowned. "I thought we were heading for the cave?"

Aladdin held up his red gem and it beamed a light through the battlefield and into the darkness beyond. "Well, it will be very hard to avoid the battle. The Cave of Wonder lays behind the horizon, past the battle lines of the Nightmare Realm."

I grumbled to myself. Battles were long, messy, and

chaotic. It was impossible to keep track of your target, and that led to mistakes. I just wanted to get to the cave.

"I am ready," Boudica said, grinning from ear to ear. "I have trained for this moment my whole life."

"Who are all these people fighting for Sekhmet?" I asked as we rode down the dune. "I've never seen so many people from the Sandlands in all my travels."

"They have all banded together against the encroaching darkness. We of the Sands love the light, and the sun. We could not stand by and allow the darkness to invade our lands, or destroy our god, after she has given us so much."

"What has she given you?"

Aladdin turned. "Herself. She pulled the light from herself and endowed us with it so we could fight the monsters."

"I guess that's something."

"And she embraced us. While the other gods abandoned their people, Sekhmet has always treated us with kindness, and love."

When we reached the battle lines, a muscular woman stepped up from her post to confront us. She was wearing a golden headdress with a screaming yellow lion emblazoned on her chest. Her eyes were lined with dark black makeup that spun into circles on her cheeks.

"Halt!" she shouted. "Who goes there?"

Aladdin stepped forward. "I come bearing two new recruits for your army, great Onisku."

Onisku scoffed and looked at us, horrified when she saw Boudica's black dress and neon strands in her hair. "You bring us an invader!" Onisku shouted, drawing a scepter. "Even now, we fight her kind."

Boudica leapt off her salamander. "I am not an enemy to you. Those things you're fighting drove me and my people out of my homeland, and forced us to retreat to the Land of Oz. I welcome the chance to fight them."

"You are all the same," Onisku hissed. "Do not dare tell me otherwise, or I will slit your throat now."

"Do not threaten me," Boudica said, squeezing the sword handle attached to her back.

"NO!" I shouted, leaping off my salamander and rushing up to Boudica as she drew her sword. "Do not hurt her."

"It will not hurt...much," Onisku said. "Her death will be quick."

"I wasn't talking to you," I replied, turning to Boudica. "We cannot pass through without their help. Please."

Boudica gritted her teeth and sheathed her sword. "You live. For now."

"Thank you." I turned to Onisku. "We wish you no harm. We only want safe passage through the lines and the ability to pass through into the Mountains beyond your border."

Onisku shook her head. "Safe passage is something I cannot grant."

"Then just grant us unsafe passage, please," I replied. "We will fight for you in the battle ahead. I am a fine warrior, and Boudica is the queen of her people."

Onisku sneered. "I have heard of you and your people. You are cowards who deserted the fight for the walls of Oz."

"I have a duty to protect my people," Boudica replied. "But now I come back to save this land. What we find in the Mountains could be the secret to all of this."

"I highly doubt that," Onisku said. "However, if you wish to die in battle, I will not stop you." Onisku whistled, and a small boy walked forward. He carried a sword twice her size. "Mesu. Bring these cretins to the line. If they try to desert, kill them."

"Yes, ma'am," the small boy replied.

I turned back to Aladdin. "Come along," I said, but I could tell by the fear in his eyes that he was considering not joining us. I didn't blame him. He trembled as I approached him. I reached into my pouch and pulled out two dreams. "We can take it from here." I held out my hand. "Just give me the gem, and you are free."

He wiped his face with both hands, muttering. "No. I'm going. I'm going."

I placed the dreams back into my pouch. "Are you sure? It is dangerous out there. More than you could ever imagine."

"I'm just scared." Aladdin shook his head. "It was much less treacherous the last time."

I placed my hand on his shoulder. "You do not have to come."

"What else do I have to live for?"

I smiled. "The same as all of us."

Aladdin nodded. "Then let's go."

Mesu waited for us without a word. When we were finished, he spun on his heels toward the front line, and started walking. "This way."

CHAPTER 32
ROSE

"This blows," I sighed. Jamil and I sat on the side of the road, leaning against the defunct car with nothing but the light from our phones to protect us from the dark, and the tow truck nowhere to be found.

"I think that's the understatement of the year," Jamil replied with her own sigh.

We had been on the side of the road for several hours, waiting to get back to civilization. We were in the middle of nowhere. I couldn't see any towns speckling the horizon. Just dirt and mountains in the distance, and a busted car behind us.

"Maybe we should hitchhike," I said.

"Do you have money for a new car?" Jamil said.

I shook my head. "I don't even have money for gas."

"Thanks for telling me now," Jamil said with a scoff. "Unless you can buy me a new car. I need this one, poor girl."

"You knew I was poor."

"Not dirt poor."

"Hello," I said. "I was living out of my car when you met me."

Jamil rubbed her arm. "Yeah, but then you moved home. I figured that was an upgrade."

I shook my head. "No, it absolutely wasn't an upgrade. I promise you that. I'm now living in a double-wide with my conniving parents who think just because my girlfriend is missing it means I'm not gay."

"Sucks."

I dropped my head between my knees. "You're telling me. I'm the one that has to live in this broken body."

Jamil squinted into the distance and pushed herself to her feet. "It's coming."

I looked over at her. "How can you tell?"

"Super vision."

I pushed up to join her. "Is that a wood nymph thing?"

She shrugged. "Something like that. I try not to brag about it, though."

A rusty pick-up truck rumbled down the road and we ran to meet it, jumping up and down so he would spot us. When the truck finally pulled to a stop, I noticed its splotchy white paint job was interspersed with mud and grime. A fat man in a tight hat and stained overalls stepped down from the cab and hobbled over to us. He was shorter than I expected.

"You call for a tow?" he said in a gruff voice.

Jamil nodded. "Yup. Our car is in the ditch back there."

He shook his head, peering behind us toward the ditch. "Zeus's beard. How did it get down there?"

Jamil kicked the dirt. "You don't want to know."

"Yeah, yeah. You were probably texting and driving again." The driver took off his cap and scratched his head. "Kids are always texting and driving around here. And then some armadillo pops out and they swerve." He mumbled as he hopped back into his truck and turned it off the road. "Stupid kids."

He never would have believed it if I told him the real reason that I swerved off the road. I wasn't sure I believed that a car with no driver caused me to freak out and make me crash, but no good could come out of a confession. It would only prove he was gullible. He could have me committed if he didn't believe me.

Jamil jammed me in the rib. "Did you see the pendant hanging around his neck?"

"No," I replied. "I don't make it a habit to study men's jewelry."

"It's obsidian."

"So?"

"It's a sign." Jamil slid down the hill toward the truck.

I didn't want to follow her. "Come on. Can't we just—"

Jamil walked up to the driver, who was busy hitching the winch to the undercarriage of her car. The pendant dangling down around his neck was in the shape of a Viking with a twisted beard.

"Nice necklace," Jamil said, pointing.

The man grunted.

"Tell me about it," Jamil said. "Is it a family heirloom?"

"No. I just like black. I found it in an abandoned car, and I liked it."

"Abandoned car? So, you're a thief?"

"It's not stealing if they don't come back for it," he said. "Most people give up and just leave their cars on the road. Most of my day is picking up strays the city calls in, and that's where I found this thing."

"Interesting," Jamil said. "And you said Zeus up there, not Jesus or God. Why not?"

"It's blasphemous to take the Lord's name in vain."

Jamil pulled her necklace out of her shirt. It was the amulet that transformed her from a wood nymph into a human. "I'm just gonna ask. Does this mean anything to you?"

"I don't have time—" The driver stopped dead when he turned to Jamil. "Well, I'll be. So what are you? Fairy, Gorgon, Succubus?"

Jamil smiled. "You first."

"Dwarf," the driver chuckled. "Well, on my mother's side."

Jamil stroked her chin. "Don't female dwarves have beards?"

The dwarf crossed his arms. "What of it?"

"Nothing," Jamil said, raising her eyebrows. "Just...asking."

He looked down at his necklace with pride. "She gave me this when I was a baby. Said my family were great miners."

"Well, most dwarves are."

The dwarf dropped his pendant back to his chest. "Even for dwarves, my ancestors were supposed to be legendary. That's what she said, of course. One day I'll find 'em, when I can earn enough from helping your ruddy lot."

Jamil stepped closer. "That's the thing. We don't have...money."

The driver laughed. "Fairy folk rarely do. Now come on, show me yours."

Jamil had never taken her necklace off in front of me before. When she did, her arms and legs became wooden, and leaves formed on her face. Her eyes turned from the brown I knew into hollow black.

"Well, I'll be," the dwarf chuckled. "A wood nymph. Haven't ever seen one of you out here in the high desert."

Jamil put the amulet back on and transformed into the plain human I recognized. "Hope you don't mind if I put this back on. Who knows what kind of people you see out here at night?"

"No bother to me." He finished latching the car to the truck. "Now, about the cost to fix this car."

I sighed. "We'll find a way to pay you. We promise."

The driver smiled. "Nah, it's okay. What I was gonna say is that your friend did me a great service, and showed great trust, revealing her true form, so I'll return in kind. This will be my good deed for the year. For fairy folk, we'll call it even."

"Really?"

He nodded. "Two fairy folks, out for a spin, got into some trouble. That sounds like the beginning of a nice tale to me. Shame if money came between it and a nice ending, don't you think?"

I smiled. "I do think." I couldn't tell him that I was just a human. It would break his dwarven heart, and who knows what he would charge us if he found out I wasn't one of them.

He tightened the winch and the car began to lift into the air. "Hop in. Let's get you fixed up."

"Thank you," Jamil said. "I've always depended on the kindness of strangers."

"Watch out for that. It'll get you in trouble one day..." There was a long pause, and then he smiled. "Not today, though."

CHAPTER 33
NIMUE

I watched the frog hop forward, slowly. It would plod along, pause, then continue on at its pace, without any sense of urgency. If I had blood, it would be boiling. We had been following the dumb frog hopping for hours and had only just gotten far enough away from Etsop's shop that I could no longer see it.

"Can't this thing go any faster?" I asked.

"I don't know," Esther frowned. "It is not my pet. Maybe you should ask it."

I shrugged. "I don't speak frog."

"And I do?" Esther raised her eyebrows. "What are you insinuating?"

"Nothing," I said. "I just thought that perhaps a lizard could speak with an amphibian."

Esther shook her head. "That's racist."

"It is not!" I said, throwing up my hands.

"It is," Esther said. "You don't get to tell me what is racist."

"Ugh," I replied. "Can we just get on with it?" I picked up a stick from the ground and used it to prod the frog. It ribbited, then flicked out its tongue and picked up an incandescent bug that floated past.

"I hate this frog."

Esther smiled. "Perhaps it hates you, too."

"Then it's not as stupid as it looks."

The frog took a great leap, and I rushed forward, following it.

"Can I ask you something?" Esther said when she caught up with me.

"If you must."

She paused for a second and pursed her lips. "What was my daughter like, when you knew her?"

I hesitated. I did not want to lie to my Gorgon friend. "She was...willful," I began. "There was no obstacle she would not overcome, even if it led to certain and immediate peril." Yes, both of those things were true. "And she had an ascorbic wit, which grated people the wrong way, but I found it delightful." That last was a bit of a lie.

Esther smiled to herself as I spoke, nodding in agreement. "Did she ever find her love?"

"Oh yes," I replied. "She saved Rose from certain doom twice, and then Rose saved her from certain doom, and then they saved each other."

"Sounds harrowing," Esther said with a chuckle.

"Quite." I said, trying not to roll my eyes. "Yes, she has a knack for escaping dangerous situations, too."

A forest full of iridescent trees rose into our view. Monstrous noises came from it, and yet, the frog leapt directly toward it.

"No," I said. "Bad frog. Let's go around."

But it didn't listen. For the first time since we left Etsop's shop, the frog hurried. It bolted forward toward the foreboding trees, croaking louder and more exuberantly with each hop.

"Are we meant to follow it in there?" I asked.

"I suppose so. Perhaps it's found Epiales's trail."

I grumbled, straightening the mask on my head. The weight of the weird skeletal headdress was making my neck go stiff. "Here goes."

"Did my daughter ever speak of me?" Esther asked as we walked toward the forest. The sounds of rumbling doom grew louder. I gulped loudly.

"Of course she did," I said.

"Then, why did you not recognize me?" she asked as we continued further.

"I...just thought it would be too big of a coincidence. After all, what are the chances that your friend's mother would save you from a hovering mouth in the Nightmare Realm?"

The Gorgon seemed satisfied with that answer. "I suppose so."

The bullfrog took one more leap and disappeared into the darkness of the forest, with only the green light from the neon stripes on its back visible for us to track.

"So, in then?" I asked.

"The only way out is through?" Esther said, slithering over a fallen branch. I followed close behind.

"Excuse me, son," Isiah said to a guard standing at the base of the temple. He was dressed in silver and wearing the emblem of a spider on his chest. Behind him, a great temple extended up into the heavens in two dozen slatted layers, each smaller than the last, funneling itself to a small dome on top. A guard stood at each of four stairways that led up to the top. "Can you please bring us to Ameyo?"

I expected the guard to slice Isiah in half, or at least tell him to move along, but neither of those things happened. Instead, the guard relaxed his shoulders and smiled. "Of course, Kofi. Follow me."

The guard turned on his heels and we followed him to a set of stairs. "Why did he call you Kofi?" I asked.

"Because that is my name," Isiah replied. He watched me fumbling with the golden book. "Do you want me to carry that now?"

I shook my head. "No. I have it." I didn't have it. "Why would you have me call you Isiah then?"

"Isiah is also my name," he said.

"I don't understand."

"Long ago, my people were brought to a new land, and stripped of their names," Isiah said. "When I was brought there, I lost my name, and they gave me a new one. I do not give my true name to any except those I consider friends."

"And you didn't consider me a friend?" I asked.

"Not at first." He smiled. "I do now, and isn't that more important?"

"I suppose," I said, readjusting the book again. "I don't have many friends, either."

"Oh, I have many friends," he replied. "And we always help lighten each other's load."

"Fine," I said, thrusting the book at him. "I suppose it won't do any harm if you carried it for just a little bit."

He took the book and studied it for a moment, turning it over in his hands. "It is quite light, considering it is made of gold."

"Well, who knows what it's really made of," I replied, rubbing my arms. "What does your name mean?" I asked.

"Friday, the day I was born. Where I am from, we are often named for the day we were born."

"I like it," I said with a smile. "It's better than my name, which means little that I care to discuss."

"That's okay. We do not have to discuss it."

I wanted to discuss it a little. There was something about Isiah that made me want to talk to him. There was a long silence as we climbed. All I could hear was Isiah and the guard panting slightly as they climbed. "Lamb."

"Excuse me?"

"It means lamb. When I was young...in fae culture, the first-born daughter is meant as a sacrifice to the gods."

"But you were not used as a sacrifice if you ended up here."

"...no. I was sacrificed. That's exactly how I ended up

here. My parents were merciful, at least. They put me to sleep before they sacrificed me."

"That is horrible."

"Yeah," I said as I rested on the top of the stairs after our long climb. "We are not so different, humans and fae, insomuch as we are both filled with wickedness."

Isiah watched the guard walk away from us. "He has gone to inform the king of our arrival."

My eyebrows shot up. "You must be very important."

"There are not many in this kingdom," Isiah replied. "We are all important. That is one thing Anansi insisted upon. Every member of his tribe is the same. We are Ubuntu."

"Ubuntu?"

"The god Anansi travelled much in his time on Earth, and he learned of Ubuntu from a tribe of people in the south of Africa. It means 'I am because we are.' It is togetherness, and that we all gain when one gains."

I shook my head slowly. "We do not have that where I'm from."

"That is a shame," he said. "But it explains a lot, too."

The guard came out of the domed building and walked toward us. "Kofi, Ameyo will see you and your companion."

Kofi pushed up off the ground. "Lead the way."

The guard brought us into the temple. In every corner, next to each of the four doors, stood a large golden spider statue, and the dome was painted with vibrant colors depicting men and spiders.

"They are the stories of Anansi," Kofi said.

I smiled. "He thinks a lot of himself, doesn't he?"

"He thinks a lot of stories," Kofi replied, studying the ceiling with a smile on his face. "We live in stories, and Anansi believes in stories more than any of the other gods.

The only way he lives is being talked about. The fact that he is bound here, away from the humans he so loves, is horrible to him."

"There are humans all around us."

"There are souls all around us, but they are ancient. He misses the bonds of humanity, of a newborn, of innocence, and hope, none of which exist in this place."

I looked over at him. "I have hope."

A painted red block of marble on the floor guided our steps towards the center of the dome where a high throne sat, gilded in the shape of two hands. A beautiful woman, as dark as obsidian, sat there upon a blue pillow. Her sheer white gown accentuated every curve of her taut body, and her brilliant blue makeup made her green eyes even more vibrant.

"Kofi, my friend, it has been too long since you have come to me," Ameyo said with a robust, hearty laugh. "Tell me, what have you brought me today?"

"I'm sorry for that, my protector," Kofi said, tipping his head. "This fairy brings news from the other kingdoms. She is the queen of the Land of Oz, and warns of a great threat to you, and our people. She wishes to speak."

Ameyo turned to me. "Welcome to the Mistreach. Speak your piece."

I fluttered forward. "Thank you, your majesty. There is a great danger coming from Agrona's Mountains. The Night-mare Realm is invading Urgu, and we must all stand against it together."

Ameyo stared at me, expressionless. "And why would we risk ourselves to protect a continent that imprisons us and our god?"

"Because there are people in it that had nothing to do with that." I nodded towards Kofi. "Your friend Kofi taught me a word. Ubuntu. We are stronger together than apart. I am because we are, and we are stronger together. We cannot defeat the Nightmare Realm without your help. Agrona is too powerful, and she hopes to bring Epiales here."

"Epiales! The god of Nightmares!" Ameyo said. "Impossible."

I threw my hands in the air. "It is happening. I heard it straight from Agrona's mouth just before I came here, and if she is successful in bringing Epiales to this place, then he will be as powerful as Hypnos. We must close the rift between the Nightmare Realm and Dream Realm before Epiales comes through it. Even with all the might of the Land of Oz, we cannot hope to beat the nightmares that will ravage the land. We must have the Mistreach, and Anansi to help us."

Ameyo smirked. "And you wish me to call him."

I nodded. "Yes." I grabbed the book from Kofi. "I offer this book from the private collection of Hera, written by Hypnos himself, as a tribute."

Ameyo smiled at me. "You speak brave words. I will try to contact my god and see if he will grant you an audience." Ameyo looked over at Kofi, who walked the book up to her throne. "Meanwhile, you will be my guest."

"Thank you, queen," I replied. "How long will it take to hear from Anansi?"

Ameyo took the book from Kofi's hand. "As long as it takes for Anansi to decide whether he likes you or wishes you dead."

I smiled a fake smile. "Fabulous."

CHAPTER 35
CHELLE

There was darkness.

Stifling darkness.

For as long as I descended.

Forever.

Until I forgot what light looked like, outside of the fire from my own hand.

There was darkness in front of me.

And darkness behind.

All I could do was keep going.

Hoping in the end I would find the light again.

Someday.

CHAPTER 36
NIMUE

"Come here, little...bullfrog?" I said, stepping into the dark, foreboding woods. The only light was the ominous neon of the other woodland creatures, and glowing fruit that hung from overhead. "Do we have a name for it?"

"Etsop just called it a bullfrog," Esther said.

"I think it should have a name. I feel stupid yelling at something without calling it by a name."

"Bad idea," Esther said. "If you name it, then it will become a pet instead of a tool."

I laughed. "I have never had a pet in my life."

"So why start now?"

"I don't want a pet. I just feel stupid calling it a bullfrog."

"And you think if you called it Frank, you would have more success? What if its name isn't Frank? You might offend it. At least if you call it bullfrog, that's an accurate description."

The minute Esther said it, the name sunk into my subconscious, and now I knew if I found it again, I would call our bullfrog Frank. Then, I would kill it for taking us through these creepy, creepy woods. I stepped over a downed log covered in glowing maggots. "What do you think those will turn into when they are fully grown?"

"Who knows?" Esther shrugged. "Probably some type of soul-eating moth."

"You think there are soul-eating insects in this forest?" I asked, squinting to find Frank the bullfrog.

"I think there are all sorts of crazy creatures in this forest..." As she spoke, a little girl in a white dress popped out from behind a tree, backlit by a white light and so ghostly pale we could nearly see through her. "Like that."

I stopped in my tracks. "That...Wow, that is creepy."

"Everything here is creepy," Esther said, staring at the girl. "Let's go around."

I put my hand up to stop her. "What if she knows where Frank is?"

Esther looked at me funny for a moment and I wondered if it was because I named the frog or because I wanted to get closer to the creepy little girl. "That's dumb."

I shrugged. "I walked into the Nightmare Realm voluntarily. My bar for dumb is very high."

"Fair enough." I took a step toward the girl, and Esther shook her head. "Oh, so we're doing it, then?"

I looked back at her. "Well, I am. You don't have to come."

She sighed. "Yes, I do. Otherwise, you'll die and then I'll feel guilty."

The vines at my feet slithered and moved out my way as I crossed over them. "Hello, little girl. We're not going to hurt you. We just want to find our bullfrog and get out of here."

The little girl looked at me, cocked her head, and her

eyes went red. She hissed at me with a forked tongue, then her mouth unhinged, and an orange flame shot out.

"Shield!" My hands turned blue and a shield rose from them, breaking the flames apart. I held out my arm to extend the shield and cover Esther. I dug my heels into the ground until the fire passed. Once it did, and the girl realized I was still alive, she snarled.

"You're still alive," she said in a sickly-sweet voice. "That's a pity."

I panted, exhausted. The shield spell took more out of me than the others and having to hold it so long drained my life force even more. "I've heard that before."

"You have magic, then?" the girl asked.

The toll it took on my body was great, but I did have magic. "Yes."

"And you aren't here to hurt us?"

"Who is 'us?'"

"Me and my friends."

I shook my head. "No. I'm not here to hurt you. I just want to find my stupid frog."

The girl smiled, her spiked teeth and crusted lips belying the sweetness of her temper. "I saw a frog hop past not long ago. Perhaps I could help you find it."

"I would appreciate that."

Esther grabbed my arm. "Are you really going to trust this girl?"

I shrugged her off. "I've trusted worse."

"Follow me," the girl said, disappearing behind the tree. I looked over at Esther one last time before I went after the girl. I didn't look back again, but I heard the Gorgon let out another deep sigh, then follow behind me.

CHAPTER 37

ROSE

The tow truck pulled up to a ramshackle gas station in the dead of night. There was nothing around except a motel across the street with a small restaurant attached to it...and desert. Lots and lots of desert.

"Sorry we're not bigger here," the tow truck driver said to us. "This is pretty much just a waystation for travelers. Once they get what they need, they go on their way."

"That's okay," I replied, stepping out of the car with Jamil close behind me. "I don't live lavishly. Can I get something out of the trunk?"

Jamil popped the trunk of the car, which was still high on the winch. I reached inside and pulled out the black box from Etsop. It was heavy, like a box of bricks.

"What is it?" the dwarf asked.

"We don't know," Jamil said, closing the trunk. "We're delivering it for somebody."

"Ah," he replied. "One of those."

"What does that mean?" I asked.

"A quest item." He snickered. "You're not the first I've seen, even this month."

"Lots of quests going on?" Jamil asked.

He shrugged. "It's the season. Just don't bring it up around Gwen."

"Who's Gwen?"

"You'll see," he said with a smile. "You can head across the street to get a room and a hot meal. They're cheap as you'll find. I should have this back together tomorrow morning."

"Thank you," Jamil said.

We walked across the street, heading towards the motel at the end of the world, surrounded by desert in every direction.

"This is where we die, huh?" I said.

"Positive thoughts," Jamil replied.

I didn't have positive thoughts, or truly negative ones. My thoughts merely existed pragmatically. We had no car. We had very little money except for Jamil's meager savings, and without a car we were in the debt of a demon without a way to deliver on our promise to him, which meant he would likely slaughter us.

Jamil pushed open the door to the motel and the bell above it jingled. A squat man at the desk turned to us.

"Good evening," he said with a crooked smile. He had deep wrinkles and small, round glasses. "Looking for a room?"

"Yeah," Jamil said, pointing across the street. "Our car broke down."

"Ah, yes. We get a lot of that."

"We don't have a lot of money," I added, ignoring the stern look from Jamil. Her eyes screamed, *Do you have to start every conversation that way?*

"Well, who does these days?" the man asked. "Don't

worry. We're real reasonable. Will you be dining with us tonight?"

Jamil and I looked at each other. We didn't bring any food. We didn't think we would be on a quest. "I guess so."

"Good, good. Well, when you go in the diner, just tell Gwen your room number and she'll add it to your tab." He finished typing on his computer and handed us a keychain with a rusted key hanging from it. "You're room three. Just go out and follow the sidewalk until you see it. Look for the number three on the door. I'm assuming you can count to three."

Jamil nodded. "We'll manage."

We walked out of the lobby. I started towards the room, but Jamil pulled my arm. "I need a drink, and some food."

"Did you hear that?" I hit Jamil playfully in the elbow. "*Gwen*. He said Gwen!"

Jamil rolled her eyes. "There are like three people in this place, and two of them are men. It was a good bet we'd run into a Gwen before long. Now, come on. I'm hungry."

I was, too, and so we walked into the diner next to the motel. It wasn't fancy, but at least it was clean. There were a couple of grungy-looking bikers in the back, and several miserable souls dotting the diner, eating their dinner in peace and solitude.

"Sit anywhere!" We heard a woman yell from the back.

Jamil slid into a booth with red patent leather seats. There was a big rip through the middle of the seat on my side of the booth. I scooted past the frayed lining pluming from it and settled near the wall.

"I hate this place," Jamil said.

"I don't think you're supposed to like it," I replied. "You're just supposed to deal with it."

From the back of the diner, a young woman about our

age stepped out of the kitchen carrying three trays. She was wearing a little white bonnet like I'd seen waitresses wear in cheesy movies, but it didn't cover her pink-streaked black hair. She moved deftly around the diner, dropping plates off at a half dozen tables along the way as if she had been doing it all her life.

She reached behind the counter near us and popped back up with two menus. "Here you go. Be right back." She handed us the menus and slid away. I stared after her, my jaw dropped.

"What?" Jamil said, looking down at her menu. "You look like you saw a ghost."

"Did you see the waitress's arm?" I asked, shocked.

Jamil shook her head. "No."

"Her arm was broken," I said. "It was in a cast."

"So?" Jamil asked, finally looking up at me. She was losing her patience.

I slapped my hands on the table. "And there was a flamingo drawn on the cast."

Jamil furrowed her brow. "*So?*"

"Don't you remember what Etsop said? 'If you find a wounded bird on your trip, don't let it out of your sight.' I think we're supposed to bring her with us."

"Great." Jamil rolled her eyes. "I hope she has money. I can only pay for one mooch this trip."

I leaned forward. "Aren't you freaked out at all about that level of coincidence?"

Jamil gave me a blank look. "No."

"Why not?"

She sighed. "This isn't my first quest."

CHAPTER 38

RED

The little boy Mesu held his massive sword high into the air as he led us through throngs of soldiers muddled around the encampment. Their line stretched on for miles, as if the whole of Sekhmet's kingdom stood against the darkness as one. A dog-headed creature helped a human with his breastplate; nearby, a woman and a sentient tiger sharpened a blade together. There was no prejudice on the battlefield, which I appreciated. Most of Oz bubbled with feuds between humans and monsters.

Small children and old men carried weapons and food through the camps, and monsters constructed tents for incoming troops. They didn't just accept each other, they didn't even seem to notice each other, except that their breast plates all shone the same emblem, that of a screaming lion.

"How did you find so many?" I asked Mesu as he led us through the camp.

"So many what?" he replied.

"Soldiers. I didn't know there were this many in all the Sandlands."

"I don't know," Mesu shrugged. "Sekhmet put out the order, and we follow her wherever she tells us to go. She leads the army herself, from the front. She has not taken a break in a hundred days. She fights with the fury of a warrior, but even with all her bravery, the Nightmare Realm's troops seem infinite."

Closer to the front line, the battlefield no longer looked like a muddled, dark blur. Now, I could make out a thick, chunky soup of arms, limbs, and faces. These were the nightmare creatures. Their eyes glowed a hundred different colors, and their tentacles spread every way as they mixed with the nameless faces of Sekhmet's troops.

Tall, thin creatures cut their way through the Sandland's soldiers, dusting them quickly. Thick, ugly blobs engulfed others. With each new death, the blob expanded anew, but Sekhmet's soldiers fought frantically, and they took down their share of the monsters.

They were brave and fearless. The horrific nature of their enemy didn't deter them, and for every one of their men that went down, they took down one of the monsters. We passed a range of archers, shooting their arrows toward the battle, and catapults flung fiery boulders towards the Nightmare Realm's soldiers.

"Come," the little soldier said without batting an eye. He could have been a hundred or a thousand. His face was smooth as a baby's yet hardened like a soldier's.

The shrieks of the nightmare monsters mixed with the cries of Sekhmet's soldiers, all mangling together into a chorus of horror and a melody of death, as we stepped toward a cadre of soldiers preparing their weapons.

"Sergeant!" Mesu said.

A woman replete in golden armor turned around. She placed her sword in her scabbard. "Yes, soldier."

The boy turned to us. "These three wish to traverse the battlefield, and ask to join your ranks."

The woman scoffed. "Three men aren't going to help you for long, especially the little one."

"Hey!" Aladdin shouted. "I can fight!" I raised my eyebrow. In the time I'd spent with him, he'd made it clear several times that he could not fight. Not even a little bit.

The woman looked at Boudica. "You look helpful. Mercenary from the Mountains?"

"Queen," Boudica replied, in a tone that demanded respect.

"Thank you for your service." The woman bowed her head. "We heard that your men were wiped out. I'm sorry."

Boudica shook her head. "Not wiped out, but severely depleted. The last of my people wait in the Land of Oz, hoping for a break in this god-awful war."

The sergeant shook her head. "There is nothing out there but death."

I gritted my teeth. "No, there is hope, but we must get to it."

"Well, I won't stop you." She shrugged. "Before you die, try to take a few with you, okay?"

I walked past her. "We're not going to die. Not again."

"That's what we all think." She looked back at her catapults, which swung one more barrage of boulders. "There's a break in the attack. Who knows when there will be another? Now is the time to go."

Boudica nodded. "Thank you."

I turned back to Aladdin. "Where is the cave?"

Aladdin lifted his red rock into the air and pointed it out at the horizon. The glint from it passed through the battle. "You can see it if you squint."

I looked where the red light pointed, and thought I

could see it, if only in my mind. "Then, let's go, if you are still up for it."

Aladdin nodded. "Please don't let me die."

I smiled. "No promises."

"War is hell," Boudica added. "There is no safety in the theater of war."

"A shame," Aladdin replied. "For that is exactly what I was hoping for. Just promise you will do everything you can to end this accursed war."

I nodded. "That we can do. Right, Boudica?"

"I will lay down my life for this war if necessary," Boudica replied. "Of that I swear."

"Then come, effendi." He stepped forward. "Let us save our people."

CHAPTER 39
NIMUE

We walked through the haunted woods for a long while, following the ghost child. She floated above the ground and her white light pulsed like a breath. A scar ran across her neck, deep and jagged, like her head had been cut off violently, though I didn't know of another way to cut off somebody's head.

We came into a clearing with a little town below us, whose aura pulsed in time with the girl's. It looked like some abandoned shanty town. The houses were small and run-down, as if they were built by unskilled labor, and rotten from time.

"We're here," the girl said with a smile that hinted at a darkness welled below the surface of her aura. She hovered down the slope and toward the first house on the right. The homes were set up in two lines, with a tall, steepled chapel at the end. "Welcome to my home."

As we walked down the empty street, I studied the silent houses. "It's beautiful, but where are the others that live in these houses?"

She rotated her neck without turning her body, until

she looked at me directly. I pressed my mask tightly against my face so she could not see through it. "They have mostly all joined the fight. The quiet is nice though, isn't it?"

"The fight?" Esther asked.

The girl's neck spun around even further until she spoke directly to Esther. "For a new home. We will have a new home soon, I hear."

"She must be talking about the monsters invading the Dream Realm."

The ghost scoffed. "I do not like that word...monster... we are just as we have been made." Her eyes caught mine, and I felt as if she saw right through my disguise. "You should not use such hateful language about yourself." She spun straight ahead, and in the middle of town we all caught a glimpse of a gaggle of children ghosts, standing in a circle. They were enraptured by something.

As we came closer, I realized that our bullfrog, Frank, sat in the center of them.

"Frank!" I exclaimed.

"Is this what you were searching for?" the girl asked.

"Yes."

She bent down and petted the frog. "We do not get many living beings around here. We are so lonely. What fun to have three new playmates."

I ran over to Frank and picked him up from the center of the crowd. They all stood and hovered into the air around me.

"No," one of them shouted.

"He is ours," another added.

"Put him down," a third said, blankly.

"I won't," I replied. "He is mine...ours," I said, catching eyes with Esther. "We need him."

"We need him," they all replied in unison.

One of the ghosts furrowed his brow and bared his teeth. They were sharpened, like the girl who led us into town, and he shrieked. In a flash, he pushed through me and came out the other side. I dropped Frank and fell to the ground, shivering uncontrollably.

"Hey!" the boy shouted. "You're a liar."

I pushed up onto my knees. "No, I'm not."

"Yes, you are." He pointed at me. "You aren't nice at all. My mother said not to trust liars."

Esther slithered forward. "Please, children. She's not a liar. She's my friend."

"Then you're a liar, too!" the boy said. "She's wearing a costume. She's a *human* under there!"

"A human!" The girl grinned. "Oh, what fun! I've not eaten a human soul for a long time."

"Nobody is eating me!" I shouted, standing up on shaky legs. "Do not make me banish you."

"Banish?" the girl said. "But this is our home. We were made here, in the minds of twisted children frightened of the dark. If anything, we should banish YOU!"

"Banish," the others said. "Banish. Banish. Banish."

"We should go," Esther said, a squeak in her voice.

"Agreed," I said, grabbing Frank and hopping onto Esther's back. "Banish!"

A blue light quaked out of me and sent the ghosts to the ground. They were not down for long. As Esther made her way away from the dismal little town, the children chased after us, their blue light speckling the darkness.

"Do something!" Esther said.

"That was doing something!" I replied. "Shield!"

The girl unhinged her jaw and spat fire at us as the shield rose. The other three ghosts joined in the fire, and the pressure from all of them was too much to bear.

"Here!" I said, handing the frog to Esther. "Hold him."

I used my other arm to help steady the shield, but even with all my power, I was not going to be able to hold off the ghosts for long. "Wall!"

The ground quaked with me as I raised my arms from the ground to the sky. The rocks under our feet lifted into the air and barricaded us from the fire...at least for a moment. Then the ghosts' fire crashed through the wall and their breath came upon us again.

My head spun and my knees knocked below me. These were powerful spells I was casting, and several at once. They drained the life force from me, and I could barely hang on to Esther as she slithered away from the ghastly children.

"Oh, for the gods' sake!" Esther shouted. She spun me around, skidding across the slick ground. As she did, she pulled the head off of our beloved Frank. Blood spurted everywhere, covering my dress. She leaned forward and bathed her hands in it, then used it to draw a circle around us, with a pentagram in the center.

"*Ad quos eieci te de sanguine innocentum rideat in quo pertinent. Et pugnes contra nos numquam iterum!*"

The circle glowed red, and a burst of light cascaded across the ground. As it passed through the ghosts, they turned red as well, and then stopped.

"No!" the girl said. "No!"

The ghosts seized up, as if drawn by a distant force, and then they fell away into the darkness, screaming as they went. When they were nowhere in sight, and we were alone, I hopped off Esther's back.

I looked down at poor Frank, split in half, and knelt beside him. "What have you done?"

"What I had to do. I am a monster, after all." Esther

watched me as I poked at the frog's decapitated body. "I told you not to get attached."

"What will we do now?" I asked.

Esther looked over at me. "I needed his blood to save us, and now we are safe."

"We are not safe!" I shouted. "We're in the middle of the gods only know where, with no guide, and nothing to tell us what to do next."

"That is not true," Esther said, dipping down to pick up a long sliver of blood. She drew an arrow on her hand. "*Ostende mihi viam ante.*"

Her hand glowed red as she spun around in a circle, before stopping dead. When she did, I noticed that the arrow had turned a light, powder blue. "This way. Come. I know where we must go."

I pushed up from the ground. "How do you know where to go?"

"Blood magic is very powerful."

"Why didn't you use it before?"

She frowned at me. "I didn't want to kill Frank. I'm a monster, but I'm not a *monster*." She sighed. "Besides, it's not like we can find blood here. Everybody here is simply a soul, and that means no blood, unless you come from the outside, like Frank."

"I see," I replied. "Well, I suppose it was worth it."

"Agreed. Now stop dawdling."

Finally, after hours of walking down thousands of stairs, there was a glimmer of light in the darkness. When I rushed toward it, the light washed over me.

I stepped into a cavern hundreds of feet wide in every direction. The pink light from dreams glowed cheerily against the walls. It was pretty, and wonderful, but as I walked through, I noticed that the light shone on piles of ashes, unmoved from the lack of wind. I walked toward an exposed wall full of tiny, glowing pink marbles. People danced inside each one, like movies, before swirling eddies whisked them off on another adventure.

"Dreams," I heard a voice from behind me. I turned to see a tiny fairy floating in my direction. The light from its blue essence combined with the pink to produce a beautiful pastel purple. "The dwarves harvested them."

I should have been frightened at the sight of the glittering fairy but judging from the way his shoulders shrank into his body as he made his way towards me, I could tell that he was not a threat. He was just sad.

"What happened to them?" I asked.

"A monster attacked them. The further they got to the core, the deeper they had to dig, and the more they upset whatever protected this place from them."

"What was protecting this place from them?"

The fairy smiled. "Me."

I raised my hands to attack. "*Ignis*." My hands glowed with the heat of a deep, bright red fire. I was ready to battle, given the need, but still, something about the fairy's gentle countenance made me hesitate.

"Please," the fairy said. "I am not here to fight you. I am here to protect you, and your sisters. These dwarves came too close to finding the Heart of Urgu and they refused to leave, so they had to be punished. It's happening more and more these days now that the Dreamers aren't coming through. With dreams at a premium, the dwarves dig deeper and deeper into the core of the planet."

"This can't be the last of them," I said, eyeing the pink marbles. "These can't be all the dreams left to harvest."

The fairy nodded. "This whole cavern was once filled with dreams as far as the eye could see. It was beautiful, but those days are gone now."

I squeezed my hands into tight fists. "And I'm here to bring them back."

"I know," the fairy said with a slight smile. "I have been waiting for you. I thought you would come sooner to restart the heart and save Urgu, but you never did."

"I'm sorry," I said. "But I'm here now."

"That is good, because time is running out." The fairy pointed at a cracked dream, dull and gray, on the ground. "There are few good dreams left, and when the dwarves pulled them out of the wall, most of them cracked and rotted like this one."

I held out my hand and picked up the gray dream. "I won't let this place die, fairy."

"Aimon," he replied.

"Aimon?"

"It means protector. I have guarded the door to the source from the beginning, and I will take you to it now."

Aimon fluttered down the path and I followed behind him, basking in the glow of the dreams as I walked past. I hoped that dreams would fill the dark cavern again, even if I wouldn't be around to see it.

CHAPTER 41
RED

"On your left!" I called out as a demonic blob with bright red eyes charged Boudica. She swerved to avoid its tentacled attack and it splashed upon the ground. We had rushed head first onto the battlefield with the fourth line of troops and immediately were confronted with monsters bearing down on us from every angle.

"Watch out!" I shouted again, this time pulling Aladdin away from a tall dark monster with sixteen arms swiping for him.

Aladdin wasn't much of a fighter, as was my initial assessment of him, but he was small, wiry, and able to avoid attacks easily. Plus, he grew confidence, even in the face of battle. I had to respect that. I thought he would crumble, but he actually had a slight smile on his face as we traversed the battle together.

"They're everywhere!" Boudica said.

I looked at the front line of Sekhmet's troops. The Nightmare monsters were attacking in full force, crashing upon them, and they looked to buckle soon. We needed to hurry if we had any hope to save them.

"Where is the cave?" I asked.

"I don't know! I don't even know where we are! I'm so turned around."

"Hold up your crystal!" Boudica growled.

"Oh, right!" He pulled out his crystal and aimed it into the air.

His movement attracted the monsters to him, and I rushed forward to provide cover. I sliced through a hulking demon and it fell under me, its green blood oozing beneath my feet. I hadn't seen blood in years. When the human soldiers died, they disappeared in a puff of ash, but the nightmare realm monsters devolved into an ooze that soaked into the ground and turned everything black.

"It's too dark!" Aladdin pulled his crystal back down. "I can't find the light!"

"Over there!" I pointed toward a ledge away from the battle. "Let's go!"

I led Boudica and Aladdin toward the ledge, fighting monsters along the way. I leapt up and held my hand out for Boudica. Once she was on the ledge, we pulled Aladdin to join us.

"Okay," I said, catching my breath. "Where is it?"

Aladdin pulled out his crystal again and aimed it at the light. He squinted across the horizon. "There! There it is!"

I followed his hand to a cliffside across the battlefield. On the rock face a few hundred meters away, I could make out a boulder covering what could only be a cave.

"We have a problem," Boudica said, pointing. "Look there."

I saw it at the same time she did. A legion of Nightmare Realm monsters stood like guards around the cave's blocked entrance.

"I think they know what we know," I said.

"It makes sense," Boudica replied. "Those stories were passed around the mountain realm. They must have reached Agrona, too."

Thousands of monsters stood between us and the door. It was mathematically improbable that all three of us would survive a direct assault on the front lines of the nightmare demons. Really, I doubted any of us would survive. "Do you think we'll make it?"

Boudica thought for a moment. "No, but I don't have any other ideas."

I leaned my hand against the rock, and suddenly I had one. I turned to Aladdin. "Are you a strong climber?"

He nodded. "The best in Agraba."

I looked over at Boudica. "Fancy a climb?"

She looked up. The cliff was a sheer face with hardly a grip, all the way to the top. "No, but I suppose it is a bit better off than barreling across a battlefield and hoping we don't get sliced in two."

I gripped the ledge. "We've done harder things."

"Not by choice," Boudica said.

"I don't think we have a choice here, either."

Boudica grunted as she pulled herself onto the ledge. "Fair enough. Then let us away."

CHAPTER 42

AINE

The grounds of Ameyo's castle were in disrepair, but then, she ruled over a kingdom of mist, dirt and grass. I didn't see one road on our way into the temple. How did they deliver goods or services? I suppose it wasn't a surprise that the ruins were derelict, save for the pristine golden spiders that adorned the walls. The sculptures were kept spotless.

"May I ask you a question?" I asked Ameyo as we walked.

"Of course, and I shall hope to answer with precision and grace, as is fitting to someone of your position."

"How do you collect taxes?" I asked. "Your people live in the hinterlands here."

Ameyo laughed. "We don't concern ourselves with that. Anansi taught us that this is a silly place, and money is not helpful for our mental health. Even the dreams you use as currency are...frivolous, here. Anansi provides all we need."

I shook my head, confused. "And your citizens are fine with that? Living in hovels, their sacred temple—" I gestured at a crack running up the wall. "Looking like this?"

"Our citizens choose to live here. The quiet of the

Mistreach gives them solitude to escape what is chasing them, and to find inner peace."

"That doesn't sound like much."

"We do not need much," Isiah said. "We do not need food or sleep, really, and we do not crave adventure. We just want to be left alone."

I chuckled. "Well, that part I understand."

"Yes," Ameyo sighed. "You are escaping a great evil."

"Not escaping," I replied. "Trying to gain support to fight."

Ameyo narrowed her eyes. "But you choose not to fight yourself."

"I am one fairy, and my people do not stand a chance against the entirety of the Nightmare Realm. Only together do we stand a chance."

Ameyo descended a set of stairs, and I followed. When we stopped on the next floor, I was surrounded by an underground prison. The cells were empty for the most part, except for a few people who looked perfectly content with their solitude, mumbling to themselves and rocking.

"Are your people really so upstanding?" I asked, my eyebrows raised. "As to not fill the meager cells in this place?"

Ameyo gave me a side-long smile, but the contempt blazed in her eyes. "I do not appreciate your tone, fairy. I have had quite enough of your insults."

"I'm sorry, my queen," I said, lowering my head. "I have forgotten myself, as I often do. My apologies. I have just barely heard any stories of the Mistreach, and your customs fascinate me."

She nodded. "Very well. Then I will tell you. These prisons are not for our people. They are for outsiders, until we decide what to do with them."

A guard emerged from the corner and opened a cell door in the middle of the room. I only realized what was happening when another collected me in a box made from iron, a vile metal that fairies cannot escape, and tossed me in the cell, slamming the door.

"This is no way to treat a queen!" I shouted.

Ameyo stared at me from behind the iron rungs. "My apologies, but we are not trustful of outsiders like you are in your kingdom."

I suppressed a chuckle, realizing I would likely do the exact same thing, and in fact had done exactly the same thing hundreds of times before. "This is not right. We don't have time—"

"We take our time here," Ameyo said, narrowing her eyes at me. "There is no hurry for anything."

"But the Nightmare—"

"Yes, we have sent a scout to look into your claims. Don't worry, your majesty, this will be cleared up soon enough. Tonight, we dine together, and then, we will decide what to do with you."

"Please." But Ameyo turned from me and walked up the steps. I couldn't believe I was trying to save the world. I should have never helped that stupid Dreamer. Having a friend had landed me in an iron prison in the Mistreach.

CHAPTER 43

ROSE

"We should tell her," I whispered to Jamil from behind my menu.

"Are you crazy?" Jamil replied. "Even if she was one of us, which she isn't, people do not take kindly to being asked to go on a quest."

I shrugged. "I did."

"You're a weirdo who dated a Gorgon...*and liked it.*"

I sighed. I really did like it. I loved it, actually, back when I could still feel love. I hoped, in that moment, that Chelle was safe in the Dream Realm, and that somehow she could find a way back to me before the end.

"Besides," Jamil said. "You remember what the tow truck driver said about talking to Gwen about quests."

"I do," I replied, rolling my eyes.

"And..."

I took a deep breath. "I think we should tell her anyway."

"You're nuts."

Gwen jetted out from the back of the restaurant carrying two plates of burgers. She smiled at the customers as she passed them on her way to our table. She set the tray down with her good hand, then put our plates in front of us. I watched the flamingo dance on her broken arm.

"There you go," she said with a smile. "Do you need any mustard, hot sauce, or anything?"

"No, I'm good. I have a question for you, though." I looked over at Jamil, who shook her head fiercely. She didn't want me to tell her, but I had to do it. My life depended on it. The deep recesses of my tattered soul burned. I hadn't felt anything like it since I came back from the Dream Realm.

"Shoot," she smiled. "I always have time for a question from a pretty stranger."

I didn't know what to ask her that didn't make me seem like a weirdo. I decided the easiest thing was to show her the box Etsop gave me and see if she recognized it as a quest item. I laid the black, seamless box on the table. It glittered in the fluorescent overhead light, and I swore a faint hum rose from it as I pushed the box toward her.

I watched her face contorting. "Have you ever seen a box like this before?"

Gwen's eyes went wide and her nostrils flared. "Oh, hell no." She threw down her tray and stomped out of the diner. I looked over at Jamil, and then chased after Gwen. She was halfway across the street before I exited the door.

"Wait!" I yelled.

"No!" Gwen replied. "I am not going on another damn quest."

"Another one!" I ran after her. She was heading towards the garage. "You've been on one before?"

She spun around. "Yeah, I've been on a quest before. It's how I ended up here, with my best friend dead, my boyfriend in an asylum, and everybody I ever loved thinking I'm a whack job. No, thank you."

I grabbed her good arm as she tried to pull away. "Wait, look. Your arm. Etsop said not to—"

She broke free of my grip. "I don't care what Etsop said, okay? I'm not going."

"Why not?"

She started to walk away. I was losing my chance. "Why won't you come with me? Because you're doing so well here?"

Gwen stopped in her tracks and turned back to me. "Are you serious right now?"

"As a heart attack." I took a step forward. I was on uncomfortable ground, but my heart was calm and collected. "Your life sucks. You're a waitress in a diner in a literal zero horse town. So...is the reason you don't want to come with me because you're doing so well here? Cuz, I have news for you."

Bluntness was more Chelle's domain, or maybe Jamil, and the taste of it stung my tongue. Still, I swallowed hard and pressed forward. Gwen choked down tears, but they came just the same.

"I almost died when—" Gwen blubbered. "I just can't— don't you understand?"

I nodded. "I understand death. I've died before. It wasn't so bad."

"What happened?" she asked softly.

I tilted my head. "I ended up in a strange land. I became a queen. Then, I was killed again, and I ended up back here, my soul cut into a million pieces. I need to deliver that stupid box to get back my soul, or something bad is going to happen, I feel it."

Gwen shook her head. She grabbed her cast and rubbed the flamingo on it vigorously. "I can't—I'm broken now."

I pointed to her arm. "Is that where you got the cast?"

"I don't even need it anymore. I just refuse to take it off. It was the last thing—my boyfriend drew that flamingo. It was the last thing...before his mind broke." She traced the bird with her finger, absently.

"I know it's hard, but you can't fix him by hiding out here."

She burst into tears. "Nothing can fix him!"

I put my hand on her shoulder. "You know that's not true. There are forces out there we don't understand, and one of them can help your boyfriend. You come with me, and I will help you, I swear it."

"How can I trust you?"

"The same way you trust anybody—carefully. I have very powerful friends, and I swear they will help you if you come with me." I didn't know if that was true, but every time I stepped closer to Gwen, my gut caught fire like it hadn't in months. I knew she had to come.

There was a long silence, then she sighed. "Fine. I hate this job anyway, but if you get vaporized, I'm not going to cry for you, or try to save you, or do any other damned thing but run away."

"Deal."

I held out my hand, and she shook it. As we stood there, me smiling and her grimacing, the wind blew. An ominous chill went through me, and I broke free of her grip.

"We need to go. Now. Do you have a car?"

"Yeah," she nodded. "I don't live in this stupid diner, but what about yours? Dale will have it ready in the morning."

I shook my head. "Can't wait that long. We'll pick it up on the way back."

Gwen chuckled. "Presumptuous of you to think you're coming back."

"We're coming back." I said it with steely resolve so deep that even I believed it, but I felt the need to repeat it for emphasis. "We're coming back."

CHAPTER 44
AINE

I spent hours in the cell under Anansi's temple. I had never been treated so insolently in all my years in Urgu. Even when I first came to the Dream Realm, the other fairies in the Enchanted Woods smelled my royal blood.

A guard came to my cell and carefully placed a pair of fairy-sized iron handcuffs inside and told me to place them around my wrists. Once I had, he picked me up with his hand. They didn't have to be so careful, though. I wouldn't have run away. After all, my goal was to petition a god. I didn't expect it to come easy. I did expect more than a kennel, though.

"This is completely unacceptable," I scoffed as he led me up the stairs. I tried to fly, but the cuffs squeezed my wrists and sent a jolt of electricity through my body. Not enough to permanently hurt me, but enough for me to know who the boss was, and it wasn't me. I hated not being the boss.

The guard led me into a banquet room where garish brown banners hung around a long, wooden table filled with delicious-looking food. At the far end of the table,

Ameyo sat with Kofi. When I entered the room, they stopped talking and turned to me.

"Welcome," Ameyo said.

"Doesn't feel very welcoming to me," I grumbled as the guard led me across the room to sit next to them. "This is no way to treat a queen."

Ameyo shrugged. "It is how we treat all intruders into our kingdom. We do not see titles here."

I scoffed. "That's funny for you to say, sitting here at this table. You sure look like you're treating yourself differently than everybody else."

Kofi smiled. "Ameyo is only the latest of our protectors. She was once a commoner and will return there once her term is up."

"A commoner ruling a kingdom?" I sneered. "Disgusting. That is no way to rule a kingdom."

"We think it is beautiful," Kofi said. "We are all raised up, and brought low, in this world, and in no way is that more apparent than with our regents. Anansi made it so."

"Then Anansi is an idiot."

"You should not talk about our god that way," Ameyo replied.

I wheeled on her. "I'm sorry, but if nobody is above this, then neither is Anansi, and all of that is stupid. People need to be ruled. They are too dumb to do it themselves."

"We survive," Kofi said.

"No offense, Isiah, Kofi, whatever your name is. This isn't surviving. It's barely subsisting. I would rather die than eat this food or live in this place," I scoffed. "But I wasn't talking to you. I was talking to the ruler, or at least this week's ruler—until she gets kicked back down to the masses."

Kofi lifted a finger, shaking his head. "That is not polite. Let me tell you a story—"

"Oh my god!" I threw my head back to the ceiling. "No more of your stupid stories. I've been locked in a cell all day like a common criminal. The last thing I want to hear is another story from a doddering fool."

Ameyo pushed away from her chair. "We are done here."

"Excuse me?" I stood on the table, pointing my chains into the air. "*You're* offended? I just sat in a disgusting cell, bereft of even a modicum of respect, and you are the one offended. That's rich."

"I am not the one asking you to shed blood," Ameyo scowled.

"No, you are the one insulting me and treating me like a common hoodlum, instead of a queen."

"We are all dusted the same," Ameyo said. "And you have no idea who you just insulted."

"No, I don't," I replied. "And the minute he is out of my sight, I will forget Kofi completely."

Kofi shook his head. "That is too bad." Sighing, he transformed from an old man to a tall, thin, beautiful man with dark chocolate skin and piercing green eyes. "I had hoped you were better than the others."

I cocked my head. "What is happening here?"

Ameyo walked toward Kofi. "Let me introduce you to Anansi, the spider-god, and our patron."

I stammered. I couldn't believe what I had done. "I'm so sorry. You don't—I was down in that prison—I didn't mean—"

Anansi stepped forward. "You are judged by how you deal with the least of us, in your worst moments." He grimaced. "You have been found lacking. It is unfortunate."

I didn't need the wrath of a second god coming down on me. I tried to vanish, but the chains shocked me and I fell to my knees. I tried again, and an even bigger shock ran through me. A third time, the shock was so great I thought I would tear myself in half.

Anansi lowered himself to my level. "If you do it again, you will explode into a million pieces of ash." I heaved as he came closer. "You had so much potential." Then, he looked up at the guards. "Take her away."

I had failed.

CHAPTER 45
RED

It took hours to climb the sheer cliff face. The whole time, we heard the battle below us, the sounds of monsters being slaughtered and humans screaming. When we finally reached the top, we traversed the plateau until we stood above the blocked entrance to the Cave of Wonder.

"Well, we're here. What now?" Boudica asked. We stood there, looking down at the monsters guarding the entrance.

I hadn't really thought that far ahead. "I don't know. I suppose we climb down."

"That will take even longer," Aladdin said. "And those things will be waiting for us, blood in their eyes. That's if they don't shoot us down first."

"I don't—This might not have been a great plan."

"You think?" Aladdin shouted.

A yellow streak shot across the battlefield, kicking up dirt and exploding monsters in its wake, one after another. As it neared the cave, the blur slowed, and I saw the visage of Sekhmet. The body of a human, but the head of a lion, she shrieked into the air as the monsters guarding the cave chased after her.

It wasn't a fair fight, a god versus monsters. She sliced through a half dozen of them in a matter of a minute, leaving a puddle of black and green bile behind her. She roared as she shredded them into bits. When she was finished, she glared up at us.

"You there!" Sekhmet shouted. "What are you three doing? Running away from this glorious battle?"

"Trying to get down!" I replied. "Maybe you can help us?"

"Perhaps, if your heart is true," she said. "Stay there."

She motored her legs, the sand again kicking up behind her. She rushed for the cliff side, but instead of crashing into it, she turned her body and ran up the side of the rock, jumped up into the air, and landed in front of us.

"You do not look like my troops," she said. "Now I ask you again. Are you trying to escape our glorious moment of victory?"

Boudica shook her head. "We are not cowards. We came from the Land of Oz, on a quest to end this war."

Sekhmet sneered. "The only way to end this war is through bloodshed, or black-bile-shed, as the case may be."

"There is another way." I shook my head and pointed to the cave's entrance. "We believe we have found Hypnos."

"Impossible," Sekhmet said with a chuckle. "I sealed that cave myself. The power inside is too much for the world to use. Only a god can open it, and none in Urgu are as strong as me. I assure you Hypnos is not inside."

Gods had a way of overlooking their weaknesses, and Sekhmet was no exception. "Are you sure?" I asked. "This is desperate."

She nodded. "I could barely contain it myself when we

fought. I am very certain of what lies inside the cave below."

I stepped forward. "If it's that powerful, then we must try. Perhaps it is the weapon we seek."

Sekhmet thought for a moment. "I have long considered that."

"If this cave has the power to end this, it's time for us to try."

"Perhaps you are right, and it is time. I feared this day would come, when I would have to return here, but I hoped it would not be this day." Sekhmet looked out over the horizon. "My people die, and their numbers dwindle. We will never win at this pace. Perhaps—may I touch you?"

I nodded. "If you must."

Sekhmet stared at me for a moment, before taking a step toward me and placing her hand on my heart. I had never been touched by a god before. I thought she would burst me in half, but she did not hurt me. She simply closed her eyes and hummed.

After a moment she opened them again. "You are pure of heart."

"Thank you."

She turned to Boudica and did the same. "You are pure of heart as well. You have a warrior's soul."

"I know," Boudica replied without a hint of sarcasm.

Finally, she turned to Aladdin, and placed her hand on his heart. "Your soul is tainted, little one. Your ambition is faulty. I'm sorry, but I will not allow you to enter the cave."

"Not fair!" Aladdin said. "I'm the one that brought them here."

Sehkmet shook her head. "Life is not fair, little one, and war is even less fair. Only a pure heart has a chance of containing the beast that rests inside this place. It will try to destroy your will and corrupt you, but if you have a pure will, and a warrior's spirit, you can overtake it and use its power to stop this war."

"And what of Hypnos?" I asked.

"I'm sorry," Sekhmet said, looking out into the darkened battlefield, and the slaughter of her people. "None are more powerful than me in this place, and thus, none can break my wards. Hypnos is not inside. What is inside will try to break you, but you are right. It just might save this place. Do you still wish to proceed?"

I looked over at Boudica, disappointed, but resolute. "We do."

"Very well."

Sekhmet picked us up and ran us down the hill until we stood in front of the cave entrance. She walked up to the boulder, placing her hand upon it. "*Aftah ya samsam.*"

"Really?" Boudica said, chuckling.

"What?" I asked.

"It's 'open sesame' in Arabic, like the old children's book."

"My spells are not complicated," Sekhmet said. "Only powerful. I will close the door behind you, and I will wait here to open it again for you."

There was a great rumble under us, and the boulder rolled away, revealing a dark cave behind it. I took a step forward with Boudica into the darkness, and then another. Once we were inside the cave, I felt the rumble again, and we were alone.

"That sucks about Hypnos, huh?" Boudica said.

I nodded. "Let's just hope whatever we find here is powerful enough to help us. Otherwise, without some sort of miracle, we are all doomed."

"Miracles are just misunderstood magic," Boudica said, walking forward.

I fell into step behind her. "Even the most common magic in the world is likely misunderstood. Let us hope this magic will save us."

"Let us hope."

CHAPTER 46

NIMUE

We followed Esther's blood magic through the Nightmare Realm until we came upon a lava tube cutting through the plains around it, high enough for a full-grown man to walk through with ease. We heard something breathing through the cracked path, so deep it made the hairs on my neck stand on end.

"This is it," Esther said.

I glanced at her. "You first."

Unlike the rest of the Nightmare realm, where neon trees and stars speckled the landscape, there was nothing but blackness in this tube. The walls of the tube were cracked and blistered, as if it had been the scene of a great battle. I felt certain it was the end of our journey, and I stepped inside with intense trepidation, each step more reluctant.

I looked backward to see Esther following me inside. "You don't have to come."

"I never had to come."

She was my friend; a real friend, even if it was predicated on a lie. We had seen too much together, saved each other. Our bond was stronger than any I had made in Urgu in the past thousand years.

Before I was a queen, or a consort of the goddess Hera, I had a friend. She was my best friend. We told each other everything.

What was her name?

Glen—

Gild—

Gra—

Grace. Yes, that was it. Her name was Grace. We told each other everything, until my ambition got the better of me and I left her for the companionship of a god. It seemed, in my youth, the prudent choice, but perhaps blind ambition was folly.

What did it give me, after all?

I had been chased out of my castle, stripped of my power, and sent begging to a god who had me travel into the bowels of the Nightmare Realm. However, it did bring me to Esther...and now I had no choice but to betray her to get what I truly wanted, a return to Earth.

Earth. The single thing that had dominated my focus for hundreds of years, and it was within my grasp, if I could survive the horrors of the lava tube and a meeting with the Nightmare King.

"Who is there?" a voice grumbled. "Are you back to gloat, brother?"

Silence.

"SPEAK!"

"Light," I spoke under my breath, and my hands went aglow with a white light. Chains rattled in the distance. I heard them before I saw them. Great, massive chains that quaked the walls of the tube, but never gave way to the might that contained them. The lava tube rattled with another shake of their metal.

"SPEAK!" the voice demanded a second time.

"I am Nimue." I pushed the mask off my face. "I come to seek an audience with Epiales. Are you he?"

"Hrrrrm," the voice replied, bored. "A mortal. I thought it was something interesting."

"Hey!" Esther shouted. "We came a long way to see you. The least you could do was be nice about it. I doubt you have a lot of visitors here, after all."

"Come closer," the voice said. "I have not seen the light in an eon."

I stepped closer, and a pale white body became apparent to me. He was naked from the waist up, and deep scars lined his chest. His black hair was long and ratty, soaking wet like he just washed it with sewage water. Stubble dotted his long, emaciated face, and red eyes stared back at me.

"Will you do me a service, stranger?" he asked. "Would you do a service for Epiales, the god of Nightmares?"

He didn't seem like much of a god in his current state, but I believed his claim none the less. "If you do one for me."

Epiales groaned. "I will entertain it."

"Then so will I."

"My nose," he said, lifting his chin into the air. "I have had an itch for a century. Please. Scratch it."

It felt like an innocuous request, so I stretched out my hand, but Esther pulled me back. "You have no idea what wickedness he has planned."

"Wickedness?" he said. "What can a bound man do to us?"

"He is no man," Esther said. "That is a god. They are capable of anything."

I decided to be careful. I whispered "branch" and a long branch grew from my hand. I used it to rub the tip of Epiales's nose, and he groaned with relief.

"Thank you," he said when I had finished. "Now, what brings you here, magician?"

I stared at him for a long moment, looking for what Agrona saw in him. I had trouble believing she could love one so feeble. "Agrona sent me to free you."

"My beloved." His voice rose unexpectedly. "How fares she?"

"She looked...fine when I saw her." *Did she, though?* Her eyes were bright white saucers, and she wore the crazed look like a raving madwoman. "She keeps the portal to the Nightmare Realm open for you to attack the Dream Realm."

"She waits for me," Epiales said. "Well, what are you standing around for?" He rattled his chains. "Let me out."

"Not so fast," I said, holding up my hands. "If you are to be free, I have my conditions."

"And I have mine," Esther said.

I looked back at Esther. "You first."

The Gorgon slithered forward. "I demand that you allow the Dreamers here to rest, and don't take your wrath out on them. Give them a place they can be safe, and a way to find me when they come into this realm."

"Hrm," Epiales grunted, before turning to me. "And what of you?"

I sighed. "I am dying. I have the power of a human touched by the gods, but not the blessing of one. Without the blessing of a god, I cannot live long with these powers. Every time I use them, I am more broken apart."

"You're dying?" Esther said, shocked. "Why did you not tell me?"

"It's nothing," I replied with a smile. "I knew we would find a way to stop it, and now we have."

"You are friends?" Epiales said.

"We are," I said, waiting for confirmation from Esther. "At least I think we are."

"We are," she nodded. "Thicker than friends. We are family. We have done battle together and saved each other from certain death."

Epiales laughed. "Family. How trite? Do you know how I wound up here?"

"No."

"My brother found out I was going to invade the Dream Realm and came here to beg me to stop. He said we could compromise, but I would not hear of it. Our mother always favored him, even though I was the wiser, stronger brother. She gave him the Dream Realm, with an enormous continent to play with. Meanwhile I was stuck here in this filth, ruling the wastelands.

"And what did he do with his great paradise? He used it as a prison for the souls of those who dared go against the gods. It was a travesty, and I wouldn't hear of parlaying with him unless he set the gods free. He refused, we fought...he won—by cheating, mind you—and he bound me here. However, I had the last laugh. At the last instant, I banished him from the Dream Realm, leaving his kingdom in disarray so he would never see his precious Dreamers again. So, you see, family bonds mean little to me."

"Be that as it may," I said. "Those are our conditions. A safe haven for her, and a blessing for me."

Epiales laughed. "Very well. To prove that family is worthless, I'll tell you what I will do, because this amuses me. I will grant one wish. Only one. To the one who survives a fight with the other."

"What?" I said. "No way!"

"I would never!" Esther said.

"Please," Epiales said to me "She is a monster." And then he turned to Esther. "You think Nimue is a good person. You want to believe she is kind, but I can smell the treachery on her. She was bound to Hera."

"Hera!" Esther exclaimed. "Is that true?"

I sighed. "Yes, for a time, but let me explain—"

"That makes you...that makes you the Wicked Witch."

"No," I said. "I mean, I am Nimue, but I never liked that name."

"You are the most vile creature in all of Urgu. You captured my Chelle's paramour..." Her eyes darted across my face and I could see her thoughts racing as she connected the dots. "Were you even friends with her?"

I looked down at the ground. "I knew her."

It all clicked in Esther's mind, and I could see in her eyes that she understood everything. "I smelled her on you because you were enemies, not friends."

"I—please—let me—"

Esther turned to Epiales. "Very well. I accept your terms."

"Excellent," Epiales said with a grin. "This will be fun. The first fun I've had in an epoch."

CHAPTER 47

ROSE

"Seriously," Gwen said from the driver's seat of her beat up Nissan Altima. It was so old it still had a tape deck, which was jammed with goop and covered in a thick layer of dust. "What kind of quest ends in Reno?"

"A dumb one," Jamil said from the back seat. "The kind that makes me leave my car with a dwarf and hitch a ride with a stranger."

"Truth," I added.

"I'm not talking to you," Jamil grumbled.

"Fair enough, except you are."

"Yeah, well, I don't wanna be," Jamil said, kicking the back of my chair. "I just want to go back and be away from this new chick, no offense."

"Oh, none taken," Gwen said. "Questing sucks. I guess in this scenario, though, I'm not joining you as much as you are joining me, huh? Since I have the car."

"No," Jamil said. "It just feels that way."

"Why is this so important to you, anyway?" she asked, looking back at Jamil through her rear-view mirror.

"It's not important to me," Jamil scoffed. "It's important to Rose."

"Fine." Gwen side-eyed me. "Why is this quest so important to you?"

I'd already filled her in on the details of the delivery, but not why it mattered to me. I only told her it was important that we get the package to its intended destination as quickly as possible.

"It's stupid."

"This whole thing is stupid," Jamil said. "We already established that part."

"Can you just tell me already?" Gwen shouted, exasperated. "I already told you I was a quest girl."

"A quest girl?"

"Yeah," she nodded. "The kind of girl that gods and magical creatures send on quests. You know the type: mousey, pretty—but not too pretty—bad living conditions. You know, pitiful."

Jamil laughed. "Man, she nailed you, Rose."

"Shut up!" I threw my hands up. "I'm not a quest girl!"

"It's not your fault, honey. Happy people don't quest. Rich people are hard to manipulate. Whole people make terrible heroes, because they have too much to lose. You, you are exactly the kind of messed up that quest givers eat up."

"You make them sound like monsters," I said, frowning.

"Not monsters," Gwen said, shaking her head. "Monsters can be nice. Quest givers are way worse. They don't care about you, or whether you live or die, as long as the quest gets completed. I know way too many quest girls who died from injuries they got on their quest, and nobody cared. They don't get health care, or even a shot in the arm. Just a thank you, and then the world keeps going."

"How do you know all of this?"

"There's an online forum. It's messed up. Now that you're a quest girl, I'll get you an account. I'm a moderator."

"A *forum?* That's ridic—"

Boom! The wind pushed hard and sudden against our car, as if a large fist had wound up and slammed into us at full force. It wound back and did it again, nearly sending us skidding across the road.

"Whoa!" Gwen said, trying to steer us straight. With another forceful gust, the wind had pushed us into the middle of the road, where a tractor trailer bore down on us from the other direction.

"Hold on!" Gwen spun the wheel the other direction and drove across the median, through the intersection, and into the shoulder on the other side.

The tractor honked as we skidded to a stop, safely, each of us panicking to catch our breath.

"What was that?" Gwen shouted.

Jamil and I looked at each other. "Etsop."

"Quit saying that name!" Gwen said. "I don't know who that is!"

"Etsop is a demon," Jamil said. "He's the one that gave us our quest."

"Yup." Gwen sucked her teeth. "That seems like the type. Demons love quest girls."

Jamil pursed her lips, trying to regain her composure. When her chest stopped heaving, she spoke. "He told us that because Rose's soul is broken into a million pieces, forces beyond her control will try to wipe her out to bring balance into the universe."

Gwen turned to me, eyebrows raised. "The universe is trying to kill you?"

"Yes?" I said, staring at my hands in my lap. "I guess so."

Gwen laughed uncontrollably as she squeezed the steering wheel tightly. "That sounds like the universe. I hate it so much. That's why you accepted the quest?"

I nodded. "That's one reason."

Gwen snickered. "Lovely."

"What's so funny?" I asked, furrowing my brow.

Gwen shook her head. "Nothing. It's just, when I said bad people like broken people for quest girls, I just didn't know how accurate I was. I'm right about it every single time, but in this case, quite literally."

"Yeah...well...I really would like my soul to be in one piece. I haven't been right since it got all messed up."

Gwen looked at me. "And in order to get it back together, you have to deliver this package."

I nodded.

"And you have no idea what's in that package?"

I shook my head.

"It could be a bomb."

I shrugged. "It could be a bomb. It could be a binky."

"No demon would send a quest girl to deliver a binky, even a cursed one. Whatever's in there is dangerous. You ever think that the universe isn't trying to kill you, it's just trying to prevent you from delivering it?"

I shook my head. "It doesn't matter. Without my soul I can't—" I wanted to talk about the Dream Realm, how I wanted to get back there, but I knew it would get under Jamil's skin. She hated that I wanted to return there and thought I was being selfish. "I can't feel anything."

That was true. *Just say the truth, Rose, but not all of it.*

Gwen sighed. "And you trust this demon?"

Jamil shook her head fervently. "God no! But he'll deliver if we deliver. That's their code. You know that if you're a quest girl."

"It's true. It's a messed-up logic, but they are bound to it. Magic is so dumb." Gwen took her foot off the gas and turned back onto the road. "All right. Let's deliver that package."

"You're not mad?" I asked.

"No," Gwen said. "You were right. This was the most fun I've had in a long time. I have a little secret too, though."

"What's that?"

"Deep down, I love being a quest girl. At least when I'm on a quest, my life has purpose."

I smiled. I knew exactly what she meant. Gods and magical creatures might be capricious, but at least it was nice to be wanted for something—to know that you are good for something, even if that thing is dying.

CHAPTER 48
CHELLE

"Am I going to die?" I followed Aimon through the empty caverns that used to hold Urgu's dreams, toward the door to the middle of the continent, where I would try to restart its heart.

"Does death frighten you?" Aimon asked me. There was no malice in his voice, just genuine curiosity, like a question he had never pondered before.

"It does," I replied.

He sucked in deeply and took a long time choosing his words. "Then I should not answer."

"Please," I said. "Clotho and Lachesis speak in riddles. I just want a real answer, for once. Am I going to die?"

He hovered at my eye level. "I find that when people want to live, they find a way."

I shook my head. "That's not an answer."

"Because I do not know, in truth," Aimon said. "I blinked into existence here in this cavern, and was given my task by my creator, and I have carried it out ever since. I never had a choice to live or die. I simply exist."

I blinked a few times, considering this. "That sucks."

"I would love a chance to die." There was another long pause as he looked out into the abyss. "Or choose anything. At all. Just once."

I smiled at him. "Perhaps one day."

"If we survive that long."

Aimon stopped in front of a sheer wall of stone. He placed his hand on it and mumbled. The walls split open, revealing a door sunk into the wall. The same familiar snakes adorned the door, slithering in a circle and waiting for my command to open.

I turned to Aimon one last time. "I hope you get to choose one day."

"Me too," he said. "It sounds lovely."

I shrugged. "It's not so great. All my life I've been trying to escape my fate and make my own choices and look where it got me."

"You can choose not to go. You can choose to turn back."

"No," I said. "I can't. All I can do is push forward. I am a slave to the choice of others, just like you."

Aimon dropped his head. "Then I feel for you."

I placed my hand on the center of the door and took a deep breath. "Open."

The glow from my hands sank into the stone, sending tendrils of light into each corner of the door. The eyes of the snakes sprang open and glowed red. A click came from behind the door as the snakes uncoiled and locked end to end in a circle. Once they were in place, the door clicked once more and opened, revealing a bright pink glow.

"Good luck," Aimon said.

"Thank you," I said, and disappeared into the light.

CHAPTER 49

RED

The light from pink dreams lit the cave, twinkling over the golden trinkets lining the walls. There were emeralds and rubies bigger than my fist, and mounds of gold that would have boggled the mind if we were in a position to use it. It seemed quaint now to think about treasures like this when, in all of Urgu the only treasure worth anything were dreams.

Boudica knelt to examine one of the coins on the floor. "This would have been very appealing if money meant anything."

"What do you expect from gods? They think us children and have little imagination. As if these feeble trinkets could make us stop our quest."

"They might have done so," Boudica said. "In another life. Did you ever think this treasure has nothing to do with the gods and more to do with whatever malevolent force is trapped in here with us?"

"Maybe," I said. We reached the center of the room, where a pedestal rose to the top of the cave. "Nobody would put anything unimportant at the top of something like that."

"I would bet what we're looking for is up there," Boudica said, staring towards the top of the pedestal.

"I think so, too." I craned my neck to look upwards. "But how do we get up there?"

Boudica placed her hands on the pedestal and lifted herself up onto it. "We climb." No sooner had she begun to do so when the ground rumbled under her, bucking her like a bronco until she dropped to the ground and landed on her back.

"No," I said. "Sekhmet wouldn't make it that easy. Think about it. She sealed the entrance, then she filled it with trinkets to distract anybody who got through. And here, even though we've reached the center, she would not make it so easy to take her prize."

"How do we get up then?"

I searched for a way forward, but the room was dimly lit, and it was hard to find footholds on the walls.

"Let me try."

I hopped on top of a nearby mound of gold and latched onto the craggy rock. I pulled and lifted myself up the wall until I was above the pedestal and turned to see the prize that Sekhmet kept there. It was an oil lamp, just as the stories of Hypnos's capture had foretold.

"It's right there!" I said, though I was too far to reach it. "Get ready to catch!" I leapt forward, latching onto the top of the pedestal with the tips of my fingers. "Ready?"

"Yes!" Boudica said.

I rocked back and forth, until the pedestal came loose of its mooring and rocked with me. "Here we go!" I swung my legs hard and the pedestal collapsed onto the ground. As it toppled and crashed around us, I jumped off and rolled safety onto the ground. When I popped back up and brushed myself off, Boudica stood in front of me, holding the lamp in her hand.

"What do we do now?" she asked.

I stepped over to her and studied the oil lamp. "If the legends are correct, then we rub it, and whatever is inside will be released."

Boudica placed the lamp between us. "That's not very good protection, honestly."

I shrugged. "That's what I heard. Just try it, okay?"

Boudica and I each took a side and rubbed vigorously. The tarnish on the side of the lamp smeared onto my hand, but aside from my hand gathering dust and grease, nothing happened.

"Enough," I said. "Nothing's happening and I feel foolish."

"Me too." Boudica nodded. "I believe it's time to try this the old-fashioned way."

I placed the lamp on the ground. Boudica removed the heavy broadsword from her back and lifted it over her head. When the broadsword came down, it smashed the lamp into a hundred pieces that scattered across the ground.

I knelt to examine the broken pieces. My fingers flittered through the shattered remains of the lamp, but there was nothing except rubble inside.

"This is not good."

CHAPTER 50
NIMUE

I held my hands out in front of me, circling Esther as she sneered viciously, her eyes narrowed and her jaw clenched. She looked every bit the monster I always feared, but in truth, I was the monster. Now she knew what I had done—or tried to do—to her daughter and all of Urgu. Still, I did not want to fight her. She was my friend, the first I'd had in a very long time.

"We don't have to do this," I said. "Please."

"Yes, we do!" Esther said. "First you try to kill my daughter, and now you won't even do me the courtesy of answering for it? Fight me, so I am not forced to kill a coward."

"No—I just—I don't want to hurt you."

It was true. For the first time, I didn't want to hurt somebody, not even if it meant I got everything I wanted. Killing Esther would allow me to regain my life, receive the blessing of a god, and even return to Earth for the first time in hundreds of years. But I did not want to kill her.

"Fight me!" Esther slashed at me, and I dodged.

"This is your last warning," I said, molding my fists in my palm. "I don't want to hurt you, but I will."

Esther's eyes blazed orange, and I ducked away from her sight. I knew enough about Gorgons to know that if she caught me in her gaze, I would be under her control. I couldn't let that happen.

"Haze!" A mist grew between us, obscuring Esther's eyes from mine. "Hypnotizing me isn't really fair, is it?"

"What do you know of fair, witch?" she shouted. "Face me and meet your doom!"

"Then stop using your powers to hypnotize me!"

Esther snarled. "I am just using what the gods gave me. Unlike you, who is pretending at true power."

"That's not true. Hera granted me these powers initially," I said. "And the fates gave them back to me. I have been blessed with them twice and fought for them harder than you ever have for anything in your life."

"And yet, you must still grovel for them," Esther spat at me. "While I have been blessed with my gifts since birth. You're pitiful."

"Fireball!" I threw a fireball the size of a cantaloupe towards the sound of Esther's voice. Her body was mostly concealed by the haze, but I could see her shadow as she dodged my attack.

"Weak. Is that all you have?"

"Lightning!" I held out both my hands and lightning extended from them and shocked across the haze. "Lightning!"

Esther held up her arms and an orange glow materialized around her, causing the lightning to ricochet off her into the lava tube walls. "Oooh. Almost got me with that one."

I knelt, hand to the ground, trembling. I could barely contain the power anymore. "Please, don't make me—"

I heard her lunge and before I could think my hand was at my head and the words were out of my mouth. "Inferno!"

Fire flew from my hands, hotter and more intense than anything I had ever let out of me. It filled the lava tube with light and I saw Epiales smiling menacingly. He had won. The fire consumed Esther, she screamed wretchedly before she burst into a million pieces.

"You have done it," Epiales said, clapping his hands slowly. "You have won."

I knelt. "Don't speak to me about winning. The only person who has won here is you."

Epiales chuckled. "You really are a devil after my own heart."

I ripped a strip of fabric from my shirt and used it to collect the ashes of Esther that gathered on the floor. "You have no heart."

"Neither do you, clearly." He asked. "I appreciate that. What did Etsop promise you in return for those ashes?"

I looked at the pile of Esther's remains. The tears came quickly and dotted the ashes. "Leave me to my grief, for a moment."

"Fair," Epiales said. "But when you rise, do not do so with sorrow in your eyes. You chose your path, and now you must walk it. I abhor one who cannot accept the fate they themselves have chosen. Make no mistake, you have chosen this fate."

CHAPTER 51

ROSE

Gwen's car passed under a sign that said "The Biggest Little City in America," and we officially rolled into Reno, the city that probably sleeps sometimes.

"So, this is Reno?" Jamil said.

"I guess so," I said, looking up at the glittering signs that filled either side of the street like a cheap version of Vegas, which itself was a cheap imitation of every other city in the world.

"I hate it," Jamil said from the back seat.

"That's original," I muttered back.

Jamil threw her hands in the air. "Well, everything should stop being the worst."

I squeezed the bridge of my nose. "Let's just find this place and get this over with."

Gwen laughed. "I have bad news for you."

I looked at her. "What?"

She shook her head, still laughing. "It's never that easy."

"What do you mean?"

"Quest givers," she said. "They never make it easy."

"How can they know if it will be easy or not?" I asked.

"If it was easy, they would do it themselves. There's always a trick. You'll see."

Jamil pulled herself forward between us. "I have faith."

"When did you get so positive?" I asked.

"Oh..." Jamil replied. "I meant I have faith it was all gonna go pear shaped. Did I not make that clear?"

"You did not."

"Sorry," she said, feigning sincerity. "I have faith this will all go tits up."

"That's the spirit," Gwen said with a smile. "We'll be dead in no time and won't that be lovely."

Our GPS had navigated us to an address just off the main street. It was a small casino that looked like it hadn't seen maintenance since the fifties. Its façade was white—or it had been once, before it degraded into a soaked-urine color. The smell was no better. The parking lot had been mostly hollowed out by a crane that stood off to one side. We came to a stop in the middle of the dirt, surrounded by the discarded remnants of the construction crew that seemed to abandon the grounds some time ago.

The sign read "FANTASY HOTEL AND CASINO" except the F and second A were missing, so it just said "ANTSY."

"Antsy," Gwen said, looking up at the sign after slamming the car into park.

"Me too," Jamil said as we stepped out of the car. "I'm antsy, too. This whole thing makes me shudder."

"It's going to be fine," I said, grabbing the black box from the trunk. "I can't believe I have to be the optimistic one in this trio."

Gwen and Jamil followed me into the dingy building. The red carpet was frayed and stained. The brass that edged the front desk hadn't been polished in decades, so that a combination of greasy handprints and dust rested thick on it.

"Where is everybody?" Gwen asked when we reached the desk. She rang the bell twice, but nobody came. "Maybe we should just go upstairs."

I moved to the elevator and pushed the button on the wall, but it was dead. Below the button was a slot for a keycard.

"We can't," I said. "We need a key card to open the elevator doors."

"Awesome," Gwen replied, hand on her head. "The one thing that's been updated since the sixties and it's the one thing we need." She turned to me. "See? I told you it wasn't going to be easy."

"Let's just go to the casino and try to find somebody," I replied, clasping the box under my arm.

"Fine."

There was a tunnel from the hotel to the casino, and we walked onto the floor, where a roulette wheel sat empty; craps tables were overturned. Nobody sat at the poker tables. The entire place was deserted, except for the three of us.

"See," Gwen said. "I told you. Shenanigans."

"Whoa!" Jamil's eyes lit up. "This is so cool."

"Umm...what?" I replied. "This place is a hole."

"No, it's worse than a hole," Gwen added. "This is the pits."

"Do you guys really not see this?" Jamil asked with a smile. "It's awesome."

"What do you mean?" I said, scrunching my nose. "It's a dilapidated hovel."

Jamil gave me a confused look. "No way. This place is packed! I've never seen so many monsters in my whole life.

Elves, dwarfs, changelings, fire beasts...It's...it's..." She sniffed. "Beautiful. I mean, maybe they shouldn't be gambling their lives away, but this is more monsters than I've ever seen in one place before."

"What are you talking about?" Gwen said. "Are you stroking out? Do you need a hospital?"

I turned to Gwen. "I should tell you that Jamil is a wood nymph."

"Ah, well that makes sense, then," Gwen replied. "They enchanted this place so regulars couldn't find it. Shenanigans."

I turned to Jamil. "Do you think you could score a key from one of them?"

"I don't see why not," Jamil replied. "I also don't see why, either, but it's worth a shot. Wait here."

Jamil ran towards the casino floor. I watched her fading like the end of a bad movie until I couldn't see her at all. "Great."

Gwen walked toward a bench in the corner. "Not great."

"You're right." I sat on the dirty bench on the edge of the casino as Gwen brushed off her seat. "This blows."

Gwen sat next to me. "Welcome to questing."

CHAPTER 52

AINE

Anansi stomped down the hall of the prison, his loafers echoing off the stone of the walls and metal of the cages. When he reached my cell and spun on his heels toward me, he smiled.

"Hello, Aine," he said.

Anansi had shed his old man persona, and now stood before me in a tailored suit, long, thin face, and piercing green eyes. He carried himself like a god, shoulders back, head up, regal in a way even a king couldn't compare.

"Hello, Anansi," I replied from inside the confines of my iron box.

"I should apologize for the theatrics earlier. When I felt you appear in my realm, I knew I had to take care of your intrusion personally. Not everybody is given such respect. Most wander through the mists, mad for years before they reach the temple, but I thought better was needed for you."

"Thank you, I suppose."

He placed a finger on the iron bars. "I know you feel disrespected, but your position doesn't make you less of an intruder to my realm."

"I didn't intrude," I replied. "I came looking for help. There aren't any 'no trespassing' signs."

"I thought the hallucinogenic fog was enough to tell everybody to stay away. Still, you came."

I lowered my head, and my voice. "I came because I needed your help."

"Yes, you have said that. Let me tell you a story—"

"Can you not?" I sighed deeply. "Unless it's about letting me out, then I would rather you just leave."

He nodded. "Very well. Out of respect for your position, and our time together, you should know that there will be a trial so that we can decide what to do with you. Usually, it can take decades to arrange a trial, but due to your position and your sense of urgency, I sped things along."

"Why even try me?" I asked, confused. "Why not just dust me?"

"That would be unfair," he said, indignant. "Besides, given your position, the last thing we need is the Land of Oz coming down on us."

I laughed. "If you think anybody in Oz would care that I died, you have another thing coming."

He spoke in a softer tone. "Perhaps not, but I will still stand on ceremony, Aine, for the sake of your title."

My head lifted to meet his gaze. "While you stand on ceremony, people are dying—my people—and they will soon come for you."

"We will see, Aine." He spoke slowly. "I hope you are right for your sake, but I hope you are wrong for the sake of Urgu."

"I wish I was wrong. I really do."

Anansi turned on his heels. "Save it for the trial."

CHAPTER 53
CHELLE

I came through the tunnel and there it was, in the middle of the room, at the center of Urgu. Right in front of me. An enormous orb, the size of The Bean in Chicago, or a small, single story row house, twisting slowly, almost imperceptibly. The bright pink of the other dreams clustered in the cavern gave it a slight pink hue, but when I walked toward the orb and looked closely, its true color was gray, deathlike.

This was the heart of Urgu.

While the other dreams around it spun with eddies of white foam and faces dancing inside of them, the large orb in the center of Urgu remained stagnant. The memories contained in it had no life within them, just dead eyes, floating motionless, like dead fish that had yet to be fished out of their tank.

I took a deep breath. "I can do this."

I raised my hand, but it shook so terribly that I could barely keep it shoulder level without it faltering, begging to be dropped back to my side.

"I can do this."

I closed my eyes and took another breath. I thought back through my entire life. My mother cradling me in her arms, watching me play video games, forcing me to study. My first crush, who ran away from me when I revealed my true feelings to her, calling me a monster...and not even because I was a Gorgon. She called me a monster because I was a lesbian.

"I can do this."

My mother took me to the fair after that and drowned me in sugar, her serpentine body hidden under a long dress. She let me on every ride, and I ate candy until I puked. It was the best day of my young life. She made joy from something horrible. It was like magic.

I still hated that girl for making me feel like less than a human, and less worthy of love for what I was and how I felt. I hid myself my whole life. I callused my heart until I met Rose.

Rose.

She was my reason for living. She was the only good thing in my life. And if I didn't restart the Dreams and allow Dreamers back into Urgu, she would never have a pleasant dream again, and the world that she loved would fall into the hands of the Nightmare Realm.

"I can do this."

I would never see her again. All I wanted was one more moment to touch her, to make her understand what I had to do. To tell her how much I loved her. Perhaps I would see her in my own dreams.

"I can do this."

Maybe it was for the best that I could not see her before I completed my task. If she knew what I was about to do, she would stop me. But then she wouldn't be able to stop me even if she tried, and she would carry that guilt forever.

I didn't want her to feel guilty. I would gladly die for her to have one moment of happiness. Better than me having a lifetime of misery.

"I can do this."

I raised my arm again, still shaking. I could rationalize my decision, but my body knew the truth. It was irrational. It was wrong. It was stupid. But here I was, about to save the entirety of the Dream Realm.

"I can do this."

Maybe I wouldn't die. Maybe it would be fine. The fates were able to shut down the orb without killing themselves.

Of course, that kind of thought was folly.

It was much harder to create life than to kill it. Anybody could kill, but few created. Fewer created something that mattered. Few had the power to save everything with one action. That kind of power was eternal.

"I can do this."

I walked forward on wobbling legs, each step more difficult than the last. Finally, I reached the orb and pressed my hand against it. It was cool in my hand, frigid, like all dead things.

"I can do this."

I didn't want to die. I didn't want to live, necessarily, but I didn't want to die. And yet...I needed to die, so the Dream Realm could live. I couldn't believe I was about to save a place I hated.

"Uhrt—"

My hand jumped back, knowing something was wrong. The sigil. The spell was nothing without the sigil.

I made the motions with my hands that Clotho and Lachesis taught me. Fire burnt in every joint of my bones. I placed my hand back on the orb and took one last, deep breath. The room smelled of cotton candy, like the first day of the fair, and I smiled involuntarily remembering the taste of it on my tongue.

"*Uhrt Elostrnt Rtincyru.*"

CHAPTER 54

RED

Boudica and I walked back to the entrance of the cave with our heads hanging low. We both had taken a shard of the lamp, hoping that Sekhmet could coax something out of it, or tell us what to do next, but we were both feeling defeated by our experience.

"Let us out!" I shouted, banging hopelessly on the rock. "Let us out!"

"What if she's not out there?" Boudica said. "There is a battle going on, after all."

"Then I suppose we'll rot in here. At least then we won't have to deal with this war."

Boudica looked disappointed. "I like to battle."

"You would," I said.

"And I don't fear death."

"That is where you and I differ. I thought I did not fear death, but when I saw the eyes of those Nightmare Realm demons, I couldn't hide the dread that filled my stomach."

Boudica smiled. "Actually, you hide it well."

"Thank you." I nodded. "If nothing else, I have that."

I slammed my fists against the boulder again, and

Boudica joined me, shouting loudly. However, the boulder didn't budge, and we heard nothing but the muffled battle outside.

Finally, Boudica turned from the rock and slid against it. "We are stuck here."

My face wrinkled with an idea. "Maybe not. What was that thing she said?"

"There is a great evil in this cave?"

"No," I shook my head. "What words did she use to open the cave to us?"

"Ah yes," she replied. "*Aftah ya samsam.*"

I had been leaning against the boulder, and felt it shift under me. With Boudica's help, I pushed it away from the entrance, revealing the battle outside. The sound of death was everywhere.

"Red!" Aladdin shouted, rushing over to us. "What happened?"

"We found the lamp," Boudica said.

"Fantastic!" Aladdin replied.

"Not really." Boudica showed him the pieces of the broken lantern. "Nothing was inside."

"How is that possible?" Aladdin said, his eyes wide. "Sekhmet swore she bound it inside herself."

"Where is Sekhmet?" I asked.

He pointed to the battle. "Protecting her people. She could not wait for you long. She said she will be back as soon as—"

As if on cue, a yellow streak whizzed through the battlefield and came toward us. It skidded to a stop at our feet, revealing Sekhmet, with a black puddle of Nightmare Realm bile oozing behind her from the monsters she sliced along her way to us.

"Is it done?" she asked.

Boudica held up the pieces of the lantern. "It is done."

"Then where is he?" Sekhmet asked, worried.

"Where is what?" I asked. "What was in there?"

"A Djinn. The most powerful in the universe. And now, he is out, but why would he not show himself?"

"A Djinn? You locked a Djinn in the Dream Realm?" I asked.

"The gods did, yes," Sekhmet said. "The Dream Realm is powerful enough to hold a god, so the gods thought it could contain a Djinn. The other gods eventually entropized to a sort of order, but the Djinn was pure chaos. I had to stop him, for the good of the people, and lock him in that cave."

I looked at the battle raging around us, and a thought struck me. Suddenly I had an idea of how the Nightmare Realm was breached in the first place. "Maybe it has shown itself."

"How?"

"Look around! This whole thing with the Nightmare Realm invading. How do you think Agrona opened the Nightmare Realm in the first place? She would need powerful magic. More powerful than even a god. Chaos magic, maybe."

"Of course," Sekhmet said, her eyes wide. "Only a god could open my enchantments. She must have been protecting the cave so I would not learn the truth. I am such a fool."

"No, you are imperfect. Like all of us."

Sekhmet turned up her head. "I have a task for you. It is too much to ask, but I am needed here."

"Will it save us?" I asked.

"Not likely," Sehkmet said. "But it might also be the only thing that does."

I nodded. "Then I'll do it."

CHAPTER 55
NIMUE

I knelt in Epiales's prison for a long time, cleaning up Esther's ashes. Tears streamed down my face. I had never grieved anything or anyone so much in my entire life.

"Finished yet?" Epiales said, still wearing the chains that bound him to the walls.

"Don't rush me," I growled.

Epiales sighed. "It's just that...I've been here a long while, and I would like to get out now."

I sighed. It had been long enough. "Fine."

"Good," Epiales said with a smile. "Now, these are magical bracers. They do not respond to just any command. You must be strong and forceful."

"Not yet." I shook my head. "First, I want your promise that you will bestow your blessing on me, and then that you won't hurt me afterward."

Epiales smiled. "That wasn't part of the original deal."

I folded my arms across my chest. "I didn't agree to that deal. Esther did, and she's dead."

"Fine," Epiales said. "I will acquiesce to your demands. I was looking forward to flaying you, truth be told."

"Sorry to disappoint you," I said, "And you will leave the people living in the cave in the community Esther created alone."

Epiales grumbled. "Again, not part of our deal."

"I'm changing the deal. I don't have to let you out."

"I don't have to let you live."

I smiled, running my fingers along the runes on the chain. "I think you do. Unless I'm mistaken, these runes were etched to make sure you didn't escape or use magic. While you're in these chains, you are powerless."

"I can kill you even without my power."

"Then you would have already. I'm not asking much. I didn't ask you to spare the Dream Realm or anything."

"That is true," Epiales said, peering at me. "Why not?"

I shrugged. "Why would I care? I'm going on to Earth. All I'm asking is for you not to kill me, and to leave the stupid humans that Esther gathered alone, out of respect for her...and because I know how much it will hurt your pride to keep them safe."

"My pride is all I have."

"For now, but soon you will be free, and then you will have everything. Agrona, this realm, and the Dream Realm."

Epiales nodded. "Very well, for sheer spunk I will agree to your terms."

"Good." My lips curled into a sinister smile. "There is one more thing."

Epiales let out a roar. "You really are pushing it."

"Relax, I just want the answer to one question."

"Grr," Epiales grumbled. "Fine, ask it, but that will be it."

"Fair enough. Hypnos put you here. Where did you put him?"

He let out a slow chuckle. "Earth, of course."

"Is he more powerful than you?"

Epiales shook his head. "I'm sorry. I agreed to one question, and I am plum out of patience with you."

"Very well," I replied. "They're your secrets. So, you will grant me your blessing, and leave me be, and leave Esther's people alone. Are we in accord?"

He nodded. "We are. Now place your hand on each shackle and say 'break this chain.' You are gods touched, so it should recognize your magic."

I did as he instructed. When the first chain snapped, Epiales fell to the floor. I walked to the other side and placed my hands around the chain. "Break this chain."

The chain broke and Epiales was free. He stood on shaky legs, rubbing his limbs. "Thank you."

I knelt in front of him. "And now, your part of our bargain."

"As you wish."

He placed his hands on me, muttering to himself, until all I saw was white and I felt a great power surge through me. I fell to the ground. When my eyes focused again, Epiales was gone, and I was alone in the lava tube.

"Fire!" Fire burst from my hand. Instead of pain, I felt great power surging through me, more than I had ever felt before.

"Perfect."

CHAPTER 56
AINE

Eventually, after Anansi and Ameyo figured I had debased myself enough in my cell, a guard locked me in iron chains and pulled me back into the throne room, where we had begun our journey.

"Welcome," Ameyo said. "Greetings again to you, Queen Aine."

"No need for the formalities," I said, hopping off the hand of my guard. "You've imprisoned me. Me—crowned sovereign of the Land of Oz."

"Crowned, perhaps," Anansi said. "But you do not have Hypnos's blessing, and so you were not given the throne legitimately."

"No offense, Anansi, but there is no Hypnos," I said, turning to him. "He's been gone for a hundred years—"

"He came back, for a moment."

I chuckled. "And bestowed his blessing on a girl who ended up dead. I was left to pick up the pieces, so I made sure to do that as legitimately as I could. I was the crowned queen of the fairies, recognized by Ozma and Nimue, and many before them. There is no other queen in Oz except me, so I claimed the right to rule."

Ameyo shook her head. "And yet, you do not have the blessing of Hypnos, meaning you are as much a usurper as Nimue."

"Usurper!" I screamed. "There is no rightful heir to the throne of Oz."

"I am a rightful heir," Ameyo said. "I have been given Anansi's blessing."

I shrugged. "For now, until you lose your post."

"And then another will be worthy."

I smirked. "Then please, by all means, go and claim my title before you lose yours. The Emerald City has been overrun by shadow demons, and trapped by Agrona, but go ahead. If you can retake it from her, be my guest. At least then you'll be doing something for Urgu instead of just sitting here."

"We are doing our best," Anansi said.

"Your best isn't good enough!" I hissed. "It's nothing but cowardice and folly!"

"That is enough!" Anansi said. "I am a god. Show me some respect."

"Why?" I replied, spite dripping from every word. "You have not shown me any."

"I brought you here."

I scoffed. "After lying to me!"

"I had to lie to find your true character."

"And what did you find?" I asked. "I listened to your stupid stories, old man. I was pleasant and courteous. I came with gifts. And you still locked me up. What kind of character is that?"

As we shouted across each other, a giant hawk dove into the great hall and landed at Anansi's feet. Anansi knelt down next to the hawk. "My friend. What news do you bring?"

The hawk looked back at me and then to Anansi. "She tells no lies. The Mountain Realm currently battles the Sandlands. The Emerald City has fallen to shadow demons. They attack the Obsidian Spindle as we speak, trying to enter the temple. And worse."

"What could be worse?" Anansi asked.

"My spies have heard rumor of Epiales in the mountains, plotting with Agrona."

"Then it is too late," I said. "The Dream Realm will fall, and we will all be put in chains."

Anansi rubbed his face, clearly worried. "No. I do not believe that. You are right. We can rise together. Urgu may be my prison, but it is also my home. We will fight."

"Ana—" Ameyo began. "This is not the way."

"No, Ameyo." Anansi stood tall. "You are wrong. Prepare your troops."

"They are so few," she said. "They will never survive an onslaught."

"Perhaps, but we will not fight alone." Anansi turned to me. "We will need the help of Loki's people, and together we will march with the Emerald City to Agrona's Mountains and push Epiales back to the Nightmare Realm."

"Thank you, Anansi." I said. "Now, can you please get these chains off of me?"

CHAPTER 57

ROSE

"This is such bull." I sat on the dingy casino bench with Gwen, thumbing the black box next to me. "I came all the way to Reno and all I got was dirt on my pants."

Gwen giggled. She had a nice laugh. "That's being a quest girl."

I flung my arms in the air. "I am not a stupid quest girl, okay? Quit calling me a quest girl."

"I'm sorry, are you a boy?" She leaned into me. "Are you a quest boy?"

I shook my head. "I'm not a quest anything. I am a Rose on a quest, but I'm not even on a quest! I'm just delivering this stupid package."

Gwen snorted. "Delivering a package from a magical being to a magical being is a quest."

"You don't know the person getting this package is magical."

"Hello!" Gwen waved her arms around broadly. "We're in a weird casino where only magical creatures can see each other. Not only that, but I can 100 percent guarantee what's in there is magical. Probably cursed, too."

"You don't know it's magical. It could be anything."

"Right, it's probably a ham sandwich." She folded her arms over each other. "Tell you what. If you don't think it's anything, then open it."

I looked over at the black box. "I don't want to."

"Yes, you do. That's the thing about quest girls. We're good girls, so we follow orders."

"I am not a good girl."

"Then be a bad bitch."

I picked up the box and placed it on my lap. "What if it's a bomb or something?"

"It won't explode just by looking at it." Gwen slid closer to me. "Do it. Do it. Do it!"

I placed my hands on the side of the box and looked at her. "You remind me of Chelle."

"Who's Chelle?"

I sighed. "My girlfriend. Or she was. Or she is. I don't know if she's alive or dead."

Gwen blinked a few times. "And I thought my relationship was messed up."

"Oh, you aren't even in the top ten."

"Would you just open it already?"

I picked up the box and turned it over a few times, studying it. It wasn't held together with tape, or anything like that. There were no seams in it at all, so I had no idea how to open it.

"I don't—"

"Give it here." Gwen snatched the box from my hand and shook it next to her ear. "I don't think it's fragile."

"Why is that important?" I asked. Fear wiggled in my voice.

Gwen lifted the box into the air. "Because this—" She leapt onto the bench and slammed the box onto the ground. It tumbled over itself along the faded carpet.

I shot up. "What did you—"

I headed toward the box but stopped when a flap came open, and a single object rolled out. It was pink and glowing. I recognized it immediately. It was a dream, like the ones they used for currency in Urgu. I picked it up and looked at it. Inside I recognized myself and Chelle, riding in a car across the desert, laughing like Bonnie and Clyde.

"It can't be..."

"Um, Rose," Gwen said. "That's not all." She held up a sheet of paper.

"What does it say?" I asked

Gwen read aloud from the paper. "It's about time. - ETSOP" She looked at me with a confused look on her face.

"I don't get it—" I stopped talking when the room changed. Like someone flipping a switch, the room turned from a deserted old casino into an opulent one, with hanging chandeliers and hundreds of patrons in tuxes roaming around. A waiter saw me materialize out of thin air and dodged me without raising an eyebrow, as if it happened all the time.

There were elves, dwarves, changelings, and centaurs; humans with animal heads and animals with human heads. I had never seen so many monsters in one place before. I turned back to look for Gwen, but when I tried to catch eyes with her, she looked right through me.

"Stupid magic," she said with a sigh. She turned around and took a seat on the dusty bench, bouncing her leg impatiently in the air.

I couldn't worry about her, at least for the moment. The pink orb pulsed in my hand as I spun around. It seemed as if it wanted to go somewhere, so I held it before me and let it lead me through the casino.

CHAPTER 58
CHELLE

It only hurt for a moment. After that, the warmth of the orb enveloped me, pulling me into a lukewarm hug. It felt like floating, but in Jell-O rather than water. I oozed through it comfortably, raising my hands and lowering them in time with the bubbles around me, popping and growing with the dreams of thousands of people.

I saw them come upon me. Slowly at first, then in a flood. Visions of pirate ships, and dragons, and first dates, and the faces of people coming back to life.

It was working. The dreams were returning.

It was—

Pain throbbed through me. *Ow!*

It was—

Ow! A burst of fire tore through my body, as if I was being broken into a thousand pieces. The orb was heating up quickly, and my body could not take it.

Stop.

No.

I don't want to die.

Please. Ow!

The light around me turned from a pale gray into a red and finally a brilliant pink so bright I could barely look at the colors around me. Even in my horrified, excruciating state, I saw that it was beautiful.

I looked down at my fingers, but they had nearly dissolved away.

My eyes.

The pain. Oh my gods, the pain!

And then—for a moment, I experienced bliss. Warm heat washed over me, like bath water, and I felt a serene calm.

Rose.

I love you.

Then, I closed my eyes, and I was gone.

CHAPTER 59

AINE

Standing outside Ameyo's temple, I took a long look across the Mistreach and realized that it was just as horrible as everybody had told me it was for the past several eons. I couldn't see much outside of the immediate area. The trees covered the land, and the mist covered the trees. It was truly awful.

"Are you ready?" Anansi asked, walking up to me.

"As ready as I will ever be," I answered. "You?"

Anansi shook his head and looked at his feet, clasping his hands behind him. "I have not been out of the Mistreach in an age. Has the world moved on without me?"

"No," I shook my head. "Urgu does not do that kind of thing. It stays as it has always been. Anybody who tries to change it is brought down to size."

"Are you not trying to change that?" Anansi peered upwards at me.

I shrugged. "Possibly, but I like to believe I'm just maintaining the status quo. Agrona is the one trying to change things. I just want to go back to the land of Oz and rule."

"Is that all you want?" Anansi raised an eyebrow.

"No," I replied. "What I really want to do is go back to Earth."

Anansi laughed. "There we are in agreement. Even if this is my home now, we are all prisoners here."

"Perhaps one day we would both be able to leave this place."

"That is a nice dream. I like it. Perhaps when we save the Dream Realm, Hypnos will allow us both to leave."

I scoffed. "If he's not dead."

"He's not dead," Anansi said, looking out into the Mistreach. "I would have felt that kind of energy leave the universe. He is...out there. I just do not know where."

I joined him in staring into the fog. "Let us hope he comes back, before the end."

Anansi looked back at me and snapped his fingers, and we vanished. I was used to vanishing, but I did not enjoy when somebody else was in control of travel. When he snapped us back into existence, we were surrounded by marshes on either side, and the vile smell of sulfur.

In front of us, a stone temple covered in thick vines rose from the middle of the water, surrounded by lily pads and slime. Great trees twisted into the air while geysers of steam shot around us from the water. Crickets, frogs, and flies buzzed in the distance.

"Welcome to the Bogs."

"Thanks," I said, still taking it all in. "I hate it."

"Me too," Anansi said. "Be careful. Loki has a forked tongue and a wicked mind. I never much cared for him."

I perched on his shoulder. "Do you care for anyone?"

"I care for my people. Come, he rarely leaves this temple."

Anansi walked through the temple doors. Inside was even more run down than outside, worse even than the

Mistreach temple, with wild vines covering the stone walls and water dripping along the ground. The stone underneath us was uneven and cracked. This certainly didn't feel like a god's dwelling.

"Why would he choose to stay here?" I asked, wrinkling my nose.

Anansi tucked his hands behind his back and stuck out his chest, trying to look as important as possible. "Because the people who journey here mean their worship. It is such an arduous journey to get here, and if there is one thing that Loki wants, it is adulation."

We continued through the temple until we reached a small wooden door, which we walked through. Behind the door was a throne room, where a tall, lanky man with long black hair and a sullen face sat.

"Loki," Anansi said.

"Anansi." Loki stood up. "I wondered when you would grace us with your presence."

"Us?" I asked, looking around.

Loki cocked his head. "Of course, Aine. Do you think you are the first to show up on my doorstep, trying to get me to take sides in this battle?"

"How did you—" Then it dawned on me. "Oh no."

From the darkness behind the throne, a slim figure stepped out.

"So nice to meet both of you," the man said to us. He looked at us with dark, piercing eyes. "I am Epiales, god of Nightmares, and rightful ruler of the Dream Realm." He wore a long overcoat and sported a thick goatee. All of that, plus his wild and shaggy hair, made him look like a pirate. "I await your obedience."

"I will never bow to you." My voice came out as a hiss. "Hypnos is the rightful ruler of Urgu."

Epiales shrugged. "Perhaps, but he is not here, and he will not be back for a long time. I am the only one here who can bend reality to my will."

"I wish no quarrel with you," Anansi said. "I only wish the Dream Realm to be left in peace. Bring your people back to the Nightmare Realm, and we will go back to our lives."

Epiales waved a hand, dismissively. "Peace is so over-rated. Wouldn't you prefer to be let out of here? Back to Earth."

"Let...out?" Anansi said.

"Of course. My brother was a jailer, but I have no interest in keeping tabs on you or fighting with you." Epiales smiled. "We are kin, you and I, and family should not fight."

"So, we can just...go?" Anansi asked, his voice unsure.

Epiales looked down and shook his head. "Well, not yet. I may be the warden, but I do not have the key. If you help me find the way to unlock the core of Urgu, then I will let you go with me through it. I will let you all go."

"All of us?" I asked.

"Even you," Epiales said, turning to me. "It was not your fault you got tied up with Hera, and I have found her wards to be very helpful, actually. So malleable in their loyalties."

My lip curled. "Nimue found you, didn't she?"

Epiales paced slowly in front of the throne. "Yes, she let me go, and her benevolence rubbed off on me. So, if you help me, I will let you leave as well. I know every demon in Shrig." He stopped when he saw the confusion register on my face. "I'm sorry, you know it as the Nightmare Realm. I have always found that to be impolite. My denizens are no more nightmares than this place is a dream. We are two sides of the same coin, and my hope is to unite what my mother broke in twain."

"Those are flowery words from somebody who started a war," I said flatly.

Epiales chuckled. "Technically, my paramour started this war because Sekhmet refused to bend the knee."

"And she killed Hera."

"Hera was problematic from the start. She never heard a good idea except the one she said herself. Still, I mourn. Gods should not fight amongst themselves." He pointed to Anansi, then back at Loki, who was watching warily from his throne. "Neither of you are trouble." He turned to me. "Are you trouble?"

I shook my head. "I only want my people to be free."

Epiales smirked. "More than you want to return to Earth?"

"No," I replied. "Returning to Earth is all I ever wanted, from the beginning."

"Then deny them." He stepped forward and bowed toward me. "I can let you back to Earth, but only if you do not cause a fuss."

I turned to Anansi. "What should I do?"

Anansi took a few steps back. "May we have a moment, Epiales?"

Epiales lifted his hands, palms out, in an acceding gesture. "Of course, but don't dawdle, or I will take it as a sign of disrespect. I do not appreciate being disrespected."

Anansi walked toward the back of the throne room, where he took me off his shoulder. I fluttered into the air to face him. "We can't trust him, can we?"

Anansi shook his head. "No, even his mother Nox never trusted him, and she ruled the darkness."

I looked over at Loki, chatting with Epiales like they

were two old friends. "I do not think we will win over Loki. That leaves Sekhmet and you, along with whatever troops we have in the Land of Oz, against the entirety of the Nightmare Realm, Loki's army, the Mountains, and—"

"You can stop there," Anansi said. "I don't like those odds. I am not built for war. I am built for stories and tricks."

"I am built for subterfuge."

Anansi smiled. "Then I think we should use what we are good at. Let's get deeper into this beast and see what it brings us. Meanwhile, I will try my own means."

"Take it down from the inside?" I asked. "I like it."

"At the very least we can learn more of his plan and whether he can be trusted."

"Nobody can be trusted."

Anansi gave me a hard look. "I trust you."

I laughed. "That is folly, but I see no other choice but to at least trust each other."

"Then I suppose, if we must, we must."

I fluttered over toward Epiales, who smiled. "Have you made a decision? Death or freedom?"

"I choose freedom," I replied. "I want to return to Earth, and if you'll take me there, I'll go with you."

"Excellent," Epiales said, turning to Anansi. "And what of you, brother?"

"I will be ruled by none and talked down to by none. I ask you again to leave this place and return to the Nightmare Realm."

Epiales shook his head slowly. "That is a shame."

"We will see."

Anansi snapped his fingers and he was gone. Epiales looked at the empty space the god had occupied just a moment before, then over to me. "Not much of a friend, was he?"

I shook my head. "I suppose not."

"Fear not, little one," Epiales said. "I am a great friend to those who I trust."

I gulped. "You can trust me."

"Excellent," Epiales replied. "Then I have a task for you."

I bowed my head to him. "Whatever you need, your majesty."

CHAPTER 60
NIMUE

I retraced my steps through the Nightmare Realm back to
the clearing where Esther had taken me to see Etsop. This
time I did not wear a mask. I dared the monsters of the
Nightmare Realm to find me and attack me. Now I had the
power of a god and would cower to no one. As it happened,
no one attacked me. Perhaps it was because I had the
stench of Epiales on me that they stayed away.

I waited for a long time there in the clearing, and it was
quite boring. Eventually, whether it was hours or days later
I'm not sure, the shop flashed in front of me, and the back
door opened.

The side of Etsop's mouth turned up. "Did you
bring it?"

I nodded, holding up the bag. "I did."

"Then I believe we have an accord. Come in. We have
much work to do. It is hard work, binding a soul to a new
body, but what fun."

CHAPTER 61
RED

Sekhmet led me to the edge of her battle with the Nightmare Realm where a sand salamander waited. The fighting still echoed behind me, but I had a new mission; a mission that might just save everything.

Sekhmet, flanked by Boudica, gave me a stern look. "Are you sure you understand?"

I nodded. "Yes, journey to the bottom of the sea, and find the lair of Nox, mother to Epiales and Hypnos. Only she has more power than her son."

"That's right," Sekhmet said. "She has been absent from this battle since the beginning, but she watches all, and waits to take a side."

"Why not just find her yourself?"

Sekhmet shook her head. "Nox sent me here as a prisoner, and she will not hear my petition. She will hear the petition of a mortal, though, if you can find her." Sehkmet looked around. "Besides, my people are here. Earth has been lost to me for a long time, but these people are my family. They bleed for me. They die for me. I owe it to them to give them my best."

"That is noble. I will not fail. You have my word."

Sekhmet clasped her hands together. From out of nowhere, a necklace appeared in her hands. Its amulet had a golden lion on it, the same as her sigil. She mumbled into it, and when she was finished, it glowed orange for a moment. "Take this. It will protect you from the dangers of the Nightmare Realm as best it can."

I bowed my head while Sekhmet placed the necklace on me. "Thank you," I whispered.

She nodded. "And thank you."

A light flashed, and when it cleared a dapper-looking black man stood in front of us.

"Anansi!" Sekhmet said, her eyes wide. She ran to him. "What has brought you here?"

"Epiales, I'm afraid," Anansi said, returning her hug. "He has gotten his teeth into Loki."

"We must find Hera, then, perhaps—"

Anansi looked away from her. "Hera is dead. It is only the two of us against this army. I fear all is lost."

Sekhmet touched his cheek and smiled. "All is not lost, my friend. We have hope, and one who will find Nox." She pointed at me.

Anansi frowned, looking me over. "You?"

"Yes."

"This is too much to ask."

"And yet, I accept it," I replied.

"Noble." Anansi walked over to me and pulled a silver spider out of his pocket. He whispered something to it and then handed it to me. "Then you will need this. It will help you decipher truth from fantasy as you travel through the ocean."

I took the ornamental spider into my hands and bowed my head. "Thank you."

Anansi placed a hand on my shoulder. "You are the last hope for Urgu."

Sekhmet walked towards us. "You are the last hope for all of us."

I took a deep breath. "I will not fail. Of that you have my word." I turned to Boudica, who stood behind Sekhmet. "Are you sure you will not come?"

Boudica shook her head. "My battle is here. You will be fine."

"I know, but I prefer to have you on my side."

Boudica rubbed the back of the salamander after I climbed onto its back. "I prefer that as well, but our destinies are written on different parchments. I hope to see you again, before the end."

"I hope so, too. Don't die."

"You either."

CHAPTER 62
ROSE

I walked through the strange monster casino with the dream in my hand, turning where it pulsated brightest. Eventually, I found myself in front of a blackjack table being dealt by a minotaur. Two elves and a glowing fire demon sat on either side of an old man in a long beard and a white jacket.

"Hit!" he said. The bull turned over a six on his next card.

"Twenty-one!" the minotaur roared. "Winner. Wow, you're on a hot streak, sir."

"There's a reason for that," I heard behind me. I turned to see Jamil holding two drinks. "Come on, I'll introduce you."

She wasn't wearing her amulet around her neck, or maybe it was just that her amulet didn't work in this place. Either way, she looked beautiful as she led me around the table and placed a bottle in front of the man.

"Mead!" he shouted. "Thank you, my dear Jamil. What would I ever do without you?"

"You've survived until now."

"Not well," he grumbled, taking a sip of mead.

"I have somebody I want you to meet." She gestured to me and I tried not to look awkward.

The man peered at me over his glasses. I recognized his eyes even though the lines on his face had changed. "How do you do?"

Jamil smiled. "Rose, this is Hypnos. Hypnos, Rose."

I dropped the dream from my hand and stared blankly at him.

"It's nice to meet you, Rose." He smiled at me, then looked down at the dream ball rolling across the floor. "Is that for me?"

"Y-y-yes."

He knelt down and picked up the dream ball. "I haven't seen one of these in a long time." He examined it. "Do you know what this is?"

I nodded. "Of course...d-don't you remember me?"

He shook his head. "No, and I'm sure I would remember somebody so pretty."

I couldn't believe it. I thought of him constantly, and he didn't even remember me. "I—you gave your blessing to me. I was your queen. How can you not...?"

Hypnos thought for a moment. "I see the confusion. That wasn't me I'm afraid. It was...a spell I left in my absence, just in case. You were my ward, then?"

I nodded.

He cocked his head. "Then what are you doing back here?"

"I—"

"They murdered her," Jamil said. "The high priestess of the Church of the Six plunged a knife into Rose's back and dusted her."

Hypnos furrowed his brow. "Then, my point stands even more. What are you doing here? You should be dead."

I looked down at my feet. "My—girlfriend saved me... but my soul...it's broken."

"It's not broken." Hypnos placed his hand on my shoulder. "Not anymore."

A rush of energy flowed through me and I gasped for breath. A great sadness washed over me, and then elation, and then anger, but more importantly, I *felt*. For the first time in months, I felt something. I dropped to the floor while my emotions consumed me. After many long moments, they faded, and I was able to think. "You—did you fix me?"

Hypnos shook his head. "No. By coming here, you fixed yourself. And now...if you'll excuse me." He placed the dream back in my hand. "I was on a hot streak."

"No," I said, disgusted. I stood up and faced him. "You can't stay here. You have to come back."

He laughed. "Not interested."

"What are you talking about? Urgu needs you. It's nothing without you. The gods—"

He waved his hand at me dismissively. "Are their own problem."

I stomped my foot. "Excuse me, sir, but they are *your* problem."

Hypnos shrugged and took another drink. "I've been away a long time, and the Dream Realm is still there."

I marched forward, my eyes blazing. "But it's *broken*, and you need to fix it, like you fixed me."

"Forget it," Jamil said, ambling up to me. "One thing I know about meeting your heroes is that it never goes like you want."

Hypnos shook his head. "I'm no hero."

"No," I said. "You're a god. You owe us more than this, and you don't even care."

He spun around, fire in his eyes. "I do care. I wish I felt the light of dreams again. Since I've been here, I have been so dead inside, so hollow."

I raised an eyebrow. "I know that feeling."

"Dreams were the only thing I ever loved. They kept me warm. Without them, I have been adrift for a century."

"We all feel that way all the time," Jamil said, sharply.

"It doesn't matter if you have a cold, dead soul," I added. "If you ever loved Urgu, if you cared for it," I said, my voice breaking, "you would come back."

He shook his head. "They don't want me back."

"Yes, they do. Yes, we do. Yes, I do." I placed my hand on his shoulder. "It's where you belong."

Hypnos turned away. "I don't even know how."

"Then figure it out," Jamil scoffed. "You're a god, not a child."

"I—" Hypnos was silent for a long moment. Then, I watched a shockwave pull through him. His eyes moved from brown to blue and finally, pink. The same color pink as the dream ball in my hand.

A bright smile creased across his face. "The light. I can feel it. I can feel it again, for the first time in a hundred years. Something has happened! I can feel it."

"What light?"

"The light of dreams, returning to Urgu," he said, breathlessly. "I can feel them all. They were dead to me for an age, but now they call on me to return to them."

"You can feel the dreams again?"

"Every one of them. It's so beautiful." Hypnos stood up, smiling. He pressed his hands against his chest. "I feel it again, for the first time in a century, I feel it. I forgot how beautiful it was." A light washed across his face. "I know what I must do now."

"Go back?" Jamil said.

He nodded. "Yes, I will go back. Let's go save my world."

You just finished *The Fairy Queen,* the third book in The Obsidian Spindle Saga. If you loved this book, please consider leaving a review on your favorite storefront. Reviews are the best way for me to see if people want me to continue a series.

Make sure to stay reading after the author note for a preview of *The Red Rider,* the fourth book in the Obsidian Spindle Saga.

AUTHOR'S NOTE

I knew somebody had to die in this book even before I started outlining it. You can't have an entire series where none of the main characters die...or at least I can't, especially when there's world-ending stakes. I didn't want for it to be Chelle, though.

I REALLY didn't want it to be Chelle.

She was the first character I developed. She was the first character we met in the first chapter of the first book.

She WAS the Obsidian Spindle Saga as much as Rose or Red or Nimue. In fact, WAY more than Nimue, who only became integral to the plot later on.

Besides, Chelle HATES the Dream Realm as much or more than anyone. I have been known to be cruel to my characters in the past, but having Chelle die to save a place she hated seemed especially cruel, and especially perfect.

I knew I couldn't kill Rose, because she was on Earth with Hypnos. I knew I couldn't kill Nimue, because we just watched her return to Earth and we NEED to see her on Earth. It's been the build-up for three entire books. It could have been Red, I assume, but she wasn't in good position to die, really, or for her death to really matter.

No, it REALLY had to be Chelle, and I really hated it.

Plus, we ended *The Wicked Witch* with Chelle stuck alone in the Obsidian Spindle. Trapped. And lacking the conflict that was so apparent for our other characters. Her dealing with her own mortality felt like a fitting battle for this book, as every other character was fighting external demons, both literally and figuratively.

And then we had that pesky thing with her having a body.

It's funny. I didn't know when I first started this series WHY exactly her body would be important, but the moment that Atropos died in the last book, I realized what kind of purpose Chelle could serve.

I didn't want it to be Chelle, but if she had to face her end, I hope I made it such an end that you'll remember it long after you finished this book. I built the entire book around that one scene. Everything built up to it, and I hope I did her justice. Her death scene was one of my favorites to write in my whole career, and I hope you hated it as much as you loved it, because it means saying goodbye to a beloved character.

Now, I've set up all the pieces, right? Chelle restarted the Heart of Urgu, meaning that Hypnos can now return with the dreamers, Epiales has control of the Dream Realm, Red is on a quest to find Nox and stop Epiales, and everything is up in the air. The next book, *The Red Rider,* will end the first coda of the Obsidian Spindle Saga, and I can't wait to share it with you.

If you liked *The Fairy Queen,* keep reading for a preview of the fifth book in the series, *The Red Rider.*

THE RED RIDER PREVIEW

Book 4 of the Obsidian Spindle Saga
By:
Russell Nohelty

Edited by:
Leah Lederman

Proofread by:
Katrina Roets

Cover by:
JV Arts

Formatting by:
Turbo Kitten Industries

RED

The Mountain Realm.

Getting here nearly killed me.

But I arrived, and in one piece.

The army from the Nightmare Realm was formidable and hideous, but they were dumb and easy to outmaneuver on foot, especially if you weren't overburdened with other people. I had abandoned my sand salamander long ago, as the dust and dirt it kicked up gave away my position. The desert was a slog, but once I entered the hilly terrain of the mountains, it was easier to conceal my trail.

Besides, the monsters weren't looking for me, they were looking for a fight. The Golden Sun of Sekhmet's troops waited for them at the border between the Mountain Realm and the lion god's Sandlands.

From the base of Agrona's Mountain, I was sure I could see the fight raging in the distance, but it was impossible. My mind was playing tricks on me. The fighting took place beyond the horizon, two days journey behind me. Even my perfect eyesight could not make out fifty miles in the distance.

As I took a moment to catch my breath, a hot wind blew past my face. The trees above me quivered, signaling a massive monster making its way through the forest. I rolled behind an exposed rock. The branches above me snapped, and a giant molten foot smashed down onto the ground with a loud crash. Another foot smashed down in front of it slowly, plodding, without any sense of urgency. There was no need to be urgent when every step the lava golem took carried it a hundred yards forward.

Three more steps and the quaking around me stopped; the golem shrank in the distance. I didn't know what kind of beacon called the monsters of the Nightmare Realm to the border of the Sandlands, but every monster I came across was making a beeline for the battlefront. Their singular focus made it easier to avoid them.

I clasped Sekhmet's necklace tightly in my fingers and closed my eyes. She told me the necklace would protect me from the horror of the Nightmare Realm, and so far I had been safe from attack, but I would never know if that was because of my own prowess or because of the charm given to me by the lioness.

"Please, please, please," I mumbled to the charm. "This has to work. Gods of Urgu, protect and guide my steps."

There was a long way to go before my quest was over. I needed to make it over the mountains and into the Land of Oz, and then dive into the water past the Emerald City where Nox made her home under the sea, protected by the vicious mermaids. I once thought that the mermaids were protectors of the Obsidian Spindle, but had come to understand that they served Nox, goddess of the dark. They were guardians of a key that Sekhmet required to end this war between Urgu and the Nightmare Realm.

Nox was also the mother of both Epiales, god of nightmares, and Hypnos, god of dreams and true ruler of the Dream Realm. He had long abandoned us; he hadn't been seen in the Dream Realm in a hundred years. Epiales was taking advantage of that fact. In the Dream God's absence, the god of nightmares worked to take control of Urgu, and everything it touched. Without Hypnos, the only being who had more power than Epiales in the Dream Realm was Nox, and thus it was my quest was to find her. I could not fail. If I did, then we would all be doomed.

It would not be easy. Getting to the Land of Oz was hard enough. The terrain was tough and unyielding and once I managed to traverse it, I would have to climb the Wall of Itherium, a 300-foot high border meant to fend off magical beasts and gods alike, and one of Hypnos's best defenses to protect his throne in the Emerald City from harm.

There were ways through the Wall, though. I knew of one, and my friend Gyda, who lived high atop the trees in the Mountain Realm, used to speak of another that sounded like it was easier to traverse. I just hoped when I got to her house she was still there, and that I could finish my task before Epiales's grasp on Urgu was complete.

I dropped my grip on the necklace and stood, craning my neck to view the mountain above me. I could not fail. The Dream Realm would not fall while my soul stood intact. I pushed up from the ground and rushed through the gap the lava golem had made. Screams erupted from higher on the mountain as I disappeared into the trees. The monsters were still coming, and nothing could stop them, except for Nox.

NIMUE

I was sick of the Nightmare Realm. Every moment I spent on the odd, ethereal plane ruled by the mad god Epiales was one too many. And now, there were not even the sounds of the creatures that went bump in the darkness to distract my wandering mind. The demon Etsop told me they had all been conscripted to fight in the Dream Realm. Their moans had always been unsettling, but the silence was worse.

There was an odd stillness to the Nightmare Realm, too. There used to be not only sounds, but also the wind that brushed across my face and through the abundant neon flowers. The wind now was as still as the Nightmare Realm was silent.

I wanted to get out. I needed to get out. The only reason I lingered here was because of the plan Etsop devised to send me to Earth. He got the idea from Rose, the Dreamer who apparently made it back to Earth and woke up from her unconscious stupor. Most Dreamers were not so lucky as to wake up and remained in their dreams until their bodies faded away. Etsop claimed I could possess one of them, as he had once possessed a human, and lock me inside its body.

However, that required him to be on Earth to procure a body, and my soul could not transfer there without vaporizing. So, I was left waiting in the open meadow where I once stood with Esther, the Gorgon monster—at once my mortal enemy and the only real friend I had made in a thousand years—as we searched for Epiales. I killed her when she learned that I was not her daughter's friend, but her sworn nemesis.

I didn't want to kill her. In truth, I hadn't ever wanted to kill anyone, but my hands had seen much violence. While I had no bloodlust in my veins, I had a certain... survival instinct. Survival means power, and power means fear, and fear means the death of my enemies.

In a flash and a crash, Etsop's shop appeared before me. Made from mortar and brick, it glowed a haunting green around the edges, and yet, while it glowed, it did not stick out against the vibrant neon of the rest of the Nightmare Realm.

The back door cracked open, and a tall, gangly man with deeply sunken eyes stared out at me. His smile was unnatural, as if two hooks pushed up the creases on the outside of it against the will of a perpetual frown.

"Thank you for waiting," Etsop said in a scratchy voice. "It took longer than I expected."

"I'll say," I said in a snit. "It's been several days, not a couple of hours."

"Hours, days, months, years...it's all the same to me. What matters is I have procured a vessel for you. If you'll come with me, we can get started."

I followed him through the door into his haunted pet shop. Every cage rattled on my way to the back counter, each one filled with the wild, twisted beasts of nightmares. Unlike the silence of the Nightmare Realm, the beasts inside the shop cackled, howled, and rattled their cages as I passed. Perhaps once I would have feared them, but after days of muted silence, their squawks were a welcome respite from the onslaught of my own thoughts.

"Please, lay inside the outline," Etsop said, gesturing down at the floor. "Be very precise. Otherwise, it won't work." He had moved aside a shelving unit in the middle of the store, and where there used to be feed and pet toys, there was an empty space on the floor with the outline of a human being on it, drawn in red.

"Is that blood?"

"Yes, yes, dear. I'm a demon, you realize. Most of our magic is made with blood."

"I hear blood magic is the most powerful in the world," I replied, thinking back to Esther, who had shared that tidbit with me. My old Gorgon friend racing across my mind caused a twinge in my stomach.

"That it is, my dear," Etsop said with a gentle nod and gestured again at the floor. "Now, please."

I stepped into the outline and moved to the ground, sliding onto my back. I extended my arms and shifted my feet until I was perfectly inside Etsop's outline. I was a queen once, before I became an outcast lying on the floor in a pool of blood. If it sent me back to Earth, I would put up with any degradation. All I had wanted since entering the Dream Realm was a chance to go back to Earth, to feel the true grass under my feet, and to taste the sweet taste of real food; to be rid of the artificiality that made up both the dream and Nightmare Realms, where everything was a poor imitation of the real thing.

"Where is the girl?" I asked.

"Well, I couldn't bring her with me, dearie. Bodies are fragile. She would never withstand what I was trying to do to her in this realm. She will barely survive it on Earth."

"Chelle made it through with a body," I mumbled. Chelle was the half-Gorgon daughter of Esther, and she began the downfall of my reign when she entered the Dream Realm to find her girlfriend Rose, the Dreamer.

"Well, yes, but she wasn't using blood magic nor layering it with soul magic, both of which have a habit of going pear-shaped in this place." Etsop waited for a moment before continuing. "Besides, this realm becomes less stable by the day. I only hope it survives the war."

Esther had made blood magic once. She had used the blood of a bullfrog to find Epiales's cave, but it was very simple magic, not the kind of magic we were trying to execute. Instead of arguing, I decided to just smile at him.

"What kind of girl is she?" I asked.

Etsop shrugged. "You all look the same to me. She looks like you, I suppose. Or maybe not, but enough that you will be happy, I think. I'm not sure. Please don't fill my head with trivialities. I have much more important things to do."

As long as I didn't look like Etsop, I would be happy. Of course, I would never say that out loud, but part of me thought he might be able to read my mind, because a sneer ran over his face.

"Don't move," he said. "The slightest twitch could destroy the process."

"Where is the girl?"

"She's nowhere and everywhere at once. I created a pocket dimension on Earth which will pop the minute you inhabit her brain and I return to the Earth realm to retrieve you."

"Sounds lovely."

"It won't be, but she's in a coma so it makes no differ-ence to her," Etsop said. "Now that you are here and you've agreed to this, there are some things I need to tell you. First, you will be in my debt until such time as I release you. Agreed?"

"What does 'in your debt' mean?"

"It means you will owe me considerably. Usually I ask for a single favor, but this is a very big ask, so I will require your help in matters...until such time as I no longer need you."

"What if I die?"

"That matters little," he said. "You can be very helpful in death. I dare say you would be more helpful in death than in life."

I didn't have any other choice. Not if I wanted to return to Earth, and I desperately did. "Fine. I agree."

"Very good. Very, very good. Now, the second thing is that this poor girl's consciousness will not want to let you overtake it. It will fight to remove you like a virus. You must show it you belong, and that you are the boss of it. Show no mercy."

"How do I do that?" I asked, watching him pace above me.

"You seem to be very good at wielding power, from what little I know of you. Use that to your advantage, but do it more gently than I do," Etsop said, pointing to himself. "Reason with the body. Make it understand who you are and what you want with it. It is waiting for its master, and you must prove that you are better than its master. Do you understand?"

"I understand."

"I cannot help you. I can only show you the path. You must walk it."

I nodded. "I get it. I understand. Can we get on with this already?"

"Very well," Estop said with a tilt of his head. "Close your eyes. Remember, lay perfectly still."

I closed my eyes tightly. The next time I opened them, I would be on Earth. A smile tried to creep across my face, but I fought against it, heeding Etsop's warning to be still. He was mumbling over me, and through my eyelids I saw a looming brightness. I held myself completely still, and the brightness fell onto me. Its heat consumed me, and I fought against, crying out in pain. *Had Etsop betrayed me? Or was this part of the process?*

As quickly as it came upon me, it was over. There was a cool breeze and I felt the floor fall out from under me. Instinctively, I opened my eyes and saw that I was falling in the darkness, suspended by the nothingness, gone from Etsop's shop and everything I once knew. Now, I was truly on my own.

If you liked that preview, then pick up *The Red Rider* today.

Also by Russell Nohelty

The Obsidian Spindle Saga

The Godsverse Chronicles

Ichabod Jones: Monster Hunter

Cthulhu is Hard to Spell

My Father Didn't Kill Himself

Sorry for Existing

Gumshoes: The Case of Madison's Father

The Invasion Saga

The Vessel

Worst Thing in the Universe

The Void Calls Us Home

The Marked Ones

The Little Bird and the Little Worm

Gherkin Boy

Find a complete list at

https://www.russellnohelty.com/books/

About the Author

Russell Nohelty is a USA Today bestselling author, publisher, and speaker. He is the author of dozens of novels and graphic novels including The Godsverse Chronicles, The Obsidian Spindle Saga, and Ichabad Jones: Monster Hunter. He has a very entertaining newsletter, which you can join at www.russellnohelty.com. He lives in Los Angeles with his wife and dogs.

Get one of my favorite books for free at:
    www.russellnohelty.com/mail
    Substack:
    https://authorstack.substack.com
    Bookbub:
    https://www.bookbub.com/profile/russell-nohelty